RESCUE

RESCUE

JESSIE
HAAS

BOYDS MILLS PRESS
AN IMPRINT OF HIGHLIGHTS
Honesdale, Pennsylvania

For information about permission to reproduce selections from this book, contact
permissions@highlights.com.

Boyds Mills Press
An Imprint of Highlights
815 Church Street
Honesdale, Pennsylvania 18431
boydsmillspress.com
Printed in the United States of America

ISBN: 978-1-62979-880-6 (hc)
ISBN: 978-1-68437-139-6 (eBook)
Library of Congress Control Number: 2017949850

First edition
Design by Anahid Hamparian
The text of this book is set in Minion Pro.

10 9 8 7 6 5 4 3 2 1

For Rebecca Davis

CONTENTS

RESCUE

ONE
The New Girl

Joni crossed in front of the school bus, swinging her backpack.
The sky was blue, the fields brilliant green, a cool breeze swayed the sheep-shaped farm sign, and summer vacation started in just two days. Perfect! She whirled the pack all the way around like a discus thrower as she turned to wave to the driver—and there was that new girl, watching her through the bus window. As soon as Joni spotted her, the girl looked back down, so Joni could see only her hair.

No, her *hairstyle*. Who had a hairstyle in sixth grade? Nobody around here! For that matter, who started a new school so close to the end of the year?

But so what! It was time for a ride. Joni dragged her bike out of the weeds and soared down the dirt farm road. Sheep raised their heads, a gang of lambs bounced away, and black flies bobbed around Joni's face. *Yay! Black flies!* They would drive Archie into the stall, so she had a chance of catching him.

She swooped into the farmyard, scattering hens from their dust baths. Four dogs rose to their feet. The two border collies quarreled about who would greet her first. The Great Pyrenees guard dogs ambled over, wagging their tails.

"You guys should be with your sheep!"

The Bears smiled their warm brown eyes at her. Sheep were boring. They preferred hanging out with people.

In the kitchen, Joni slung her pack on a chair. Dad was already pouring her a glass of milk. "Hi, Joni Macaroni! How's my little girl?"

"Dad? Remember?" Technically, Joni was his little girl. The Big Girls were Kate and Olivia, his daughters from his first marriage. They'd graduated from college and didn't live here anymore, so it didn't matter what Dad called them. But next fall, Joni would be in middle school. What if Dad called her his little girl in public? She was training him, but he was about as easy as Archie.

"Sorry," he said. "How was school?"

Should Joni tell him about the new girl? From California, Mrs. Emmons had said, when she introduced her. From a city— San Something-or-other.

But then Dad would ask, *Did you talk with her?* Joni hadn't. None of them had, not even Danae and Alyssa, Joni's best friends, who were usually unstoppable in the talking-to-people department. The new girl stayed inside at recess, bending her California hairstyle over a book. At lunchtime, she took her

2

shiny, insulated bag to the teachers' table and ate there.

So it looked like she was shy, but that wasn't it. *Joni* was shy. The new girl was something else. If she were a store, there would be a Closed sign in the window. She wore bright leggings and a T-shirt layered over another shirt in a sophisticated way that Alyssa said was cool—but when the new girl got on their bus and sat looking at her phone, even Alyssa didn't go talk to her.

"School was stupid!" Joni said, reaching for an oatmeal cookie. "We shouldn't have to go the last week. They don't teach us anything."

Dad said, "I'm pretty sure there's a flaw in your logic. Isn't that an infinite regression? So you'd *never* go to school?"

"I'd go to school," Joni said. "Just not in June! I'm going for a ride."

"Getting ready for camp?"

"No, just a trail ride," Joni said.

"So you've got the beast under control?" That wasn't really a question. Dad was pushing, saying Joni *should* be getting ready, and he was right. Last year at camp, Archie ran away with her across the whole equestrian center and through three riding lessons. It made them famous, not in a good way.

"He hasn't run away with me since last fall," Joni said— which wasn't really an answer, but fair was fair. She shoved on her riding boots, grabbed another cookie, and she and Dad went out together.

Immediately, they were in the center of a swirl of dogs. The border collies quivered with hope. Maybe, just maybe, the sheep wouldn't come when Dad called them for milking. Maybe, just maybe, he'd need their help. They circled, watching, ready for a command. The Bears padded along, panting happily.

Dad paused by the milking parlor. "Where you heading? In case Archie comes back alone."

"North Valley Road, I think."

"You think?" Dad waited. As a free-range kid, it was Joni's responsibility to make a plan, tell somebody what it was, and stick to it. Within reason, anyway.

"Yes," Joni said. "North Valley Road."

"Okay. Have fun!"

Archie was in his stall, hiding out from the flies. Joni closed the door, slipped on his halter, and kissed his gray velvet nose. He gave her a bitter look, and she kissed him again. "What you got planned for me today, Mr. Growth Opportunity?" Carleen, her camp instructor, called him that—"a growth opportunity on four legs." He was a Morgan-Welsh cross, only fourteen hands high, which was two inches too short to be officially a horse. He looked like a horse, but he had a pony mind, cheerful and devious.

Joni brushed his white coat, put on fly spray, and lifted the saddle onto his back. Archie took a deep breath, expanding his belly so the cinch didn't even reach the buckle. He pinched his lips tight and stared straight ahead, with an inward-looking expression.

"Archie, the amazing balloon horse!" Joni led him in a small circle and tried again. "Wow, you can hold your breath for a long time!" Another circle, a third. Archie heaved a sigh. "Thank you!" Joni tightened the cinch, put on Archie's hackamore and her own helmet, and led him out to the big rock she used for a mounting block. She climbed onto it. Archie swung away so the stirrup was out of reach and stood looking innocent and bright-eyed.

Joni picked up her stick—a stalk of last year's goldenrod, actually, light and brittle as uncooked spaghetti—and touched him on the rump. Archie aimed a nip at her leg, then sidestepped close enough for her to get on. One of *those* days! She settled herself firmly in the saddle and headed down across the big front field. The hackamore didn't have a bit, but it was actually stronger than his old bridle. With luck and careful attention, she was pretty sure she wouldn't get run away with today.

Beyond that, Dad was right. She hadn't advanced much in a year. Carleen had said, "You're at the age when you should kick it up a notch. Bring some finesse to your riding."

But finesse didn't happen just because you'd turned twelve. It didn't happen fooling around out on the trails. And so what? Riding was supposed to be fun, especially after a day at school. How many kids her age would dare even get on a horse like Archie? Anyway, she had more than a week to get ready.

Archie strode along cheerfully. He liked going places. What he hated was being tacked up and handing over authority. Entering the woods, he broke into a smooth, swift trot—which Joni hadn't asked him to do, but okay. The brook trail was one of his well-behaved places. The trees on each side funneled him straight forward, so he didn't have many options.

Three big rocks marked the end of the trail. Archie stepped through the opening between them, onto the dirt road. Here, they could turn left, farther into the woods. Joni never met anybody out there, just birds and sometimes a deer. It was an easy ride.

Or, if she was feeling strong-minded, she could turn right, cross the bridge that Archie pretended to be afraid of, and ride along North Valley Road. Past the white house with the For Sale sign. Past the empty red barn. Past the little house with the ponies, and beyond, all the way to the dairy farm. That was where she'd said she was going, so that was where she should go. But was this a strong-minded day?

Not so much, Joni thought, if she could be intimidated by just a hairstyle. And that was ridiculous! She shortened the reins and firmed her seat in the saddle.

"Archie? Get your big-horse pants on! We're crossing that bridge!"

Archie pricked his ears right and left at the flowing water. He ducked his head to look at the worn boards of the bridge. For a second, he hesitated. Then, as if it was his own idea, he walked calmly across it, onto North Valley Road.

"Awesome possum!" Joni let him trot. They swept around the corner toward the white house.

On the lawn where the For Sale sign had been, watching them come, was the new girl.

TWO

Minis

Joni would have to say hi. She couldn't just ride by—unless Archie decided that's what they were doing! She slackened the reins. But Archie pricked his ears and veered toward the girl. She stood her ground, dark eyes widening, as he marched up and poked her with his nose.

Apparently, she didn't have treats. Archie sighed, yanked the reins through Joni's hands, and put his head down to graze. Joni felt her face get hot. *Way to go, Arch!* He'd made her look like a helpless dork, *again*!

The new girl wasn't looking at Joni, though. She was gazing at Archie, eyes shining. "Is he a *Lipizzan?*" she whispered.

Joni managed not to laugh. "No. He's part Morgan and part Welsh. His name is Archie."

"Because Lipizzans are white," the girl said, as if she hadn't heard.

"Lipizzans are white, but not all white horses are Lipizzans," Joni said. That was logic. Dad would be proud. "Anyway, Archie's really a gray horse. He was dark when he was born, and he got lighter as he got older. Like Lipizzans—they're not really white, either."

The girl looked up at her. "You know a lot," she said. "You're—Joni? I'm Chess. C-h-e-s-s."

"That's not what Mrs. Emmons called you," Joni said.

"No, it's Francesca, but I'm changing it." The girl was looking at Archie again, drinking him in.

"Why didn't you tell her?" Joni asked.

Chess shrugged. "Why bother, for three days? Next year in middle school, I'll start them off right . . . wow, he's *so* beautiful!"

"Yeah, he's cute!" Truthfully, Archie was gorgeous. Sometimes Joni gazed for minutes at a time at the long white eyelashes sweeping across his dark eyes. His conformation wasn't technically outstanding. His neck was too thick, his pasterns and shoulders too upright. But this wasn't a horse-judging contest. There was no need to point out Archie's faults. So what *was* she supposed to say? Should she get off? She hadn't been asked to. The new—no, *Chess*—was completely focused on Archie, and if there was a next thing to say, Joni couldn't think of it. *Why did you come to school, with only three days left? Why did you look like you didn't want us to talk to you? Are you talking to me now just because I have a horse?* Those were things *not* to say.

"Well, I should get going."

"Will you ride back this way?" Chess asked.

Joni nodded.

"I'll have a carrot for him. If that's okay. Does he like carrots?"

"He likes *everything!*" Joni hauled Archie's head up. A troubled frown came over Chess's face, and Joni's own face burned. This was terrible riding and she knew it. But it wasn't hurting him, and it was the only way. She turned Archie's head toward the road. He bent his neck, but not his body, and carried her farther up the lawn. She booted him in the ribs. He kicked up his heels in a tiny buck, just to show that he didn't have to do what she wanted. Then he surged up North Valley Road at a much faster trot than she'd intended.

Joni was sweating. Why was she so bad at talking? *And* riding! Even Chess could tell how awful that was. Now she would have to ride back past the house, and talk some more, and—

Archie pointed his ears at something ahead. Joni slowed him to a walk. They were almost at the house with the ponies, and something was going on in the front field.

The ponies had arrived at this house in early spring. The buildings sat so far back from the road that Joni had only seen them from a distance, just enough to tell that one was chestnut and one was black.

Now they stood in the garden patch harnessed to a cart, motionless, only their tails swishing. Nearby, their owner, a tall old lady in overalls and a straw hat, was hilling potatoes. Step. Bend. Scratch with the hoe. Straighten. Step. There was a long green row ahead of her, and a longer row behind, with fresh dirt piled up against the necks of the plants.

The ponies' ears swiveled, catching the sound of Archie's hooves. The chestnut nudged the black with its nose. Both turned their heads, and the chestnut pony took a step.

"Uh!" the woman said sharply. The chestnut pony placed its front feet primly together and stood still. The woman stared at him for a long moment. Then she turned toward Joni and raised one hand.

Joni waved back. But—*oh, groan!* The woman wasn't waving. She was telling Joni to wait.

She walked toward the ponies, using her hoe as a cane. The closer she got to them, the taller she looked, and the smaller they seemed. She stuck the hoe into a big tube like an umbrella stand on the back of the cart and slid onto the seat. Now the ponies looked extremely small, the size of big dogs—

"Oh!" Joni said. "They're minis!" She wasn't a huge fan of miniature horses. Some were weird-looking, and they were too small for anybody except a very young child to ride. These two were cute, though—

Archie pulled on the reins. He wanted to jump the ditch and get acquainted. Joni turned him in a tight circle, red-faced again. What was this, Ride Badly in Public Day? Meanwhile, the minis stood like little statues while the woman settled herself, arranged her reins in her hands, and reached for her whip.

When she was ready, she spoke a quiet word. The cart surged forward, and the minis came trotting up the path between the garden beds. Their eight legs twinkled, sending up puffs of dust. She brought them to a stop in front of Archie, and they turned their heads, trying to see past the blinders.

"You're the Campbell girl, aren't you?" the woman said. "I recognized that handsome pony!"

"I'm Joni. This is Archie."

"Hello, Archie. Joni, I wonder if you'd tell your father that Ruth Abernathy is definitely interested in buying two lambs. We talked about it a few weeks ago."

"Okay." No, that wasn't how Mom would want her to answer. "Yes. I'll tell him."

"Thank you." Ruth Abernathy hesitated for a second, looking Joni and Archie over with clear, possibly critical eyes. For a second, she seemed about to say something. Then she changed her mind, touched the whip to the brim of her hat like a salute, and spoke to the minis. They scudded off in a cloud of dust, with her sitting up straight behind them, so large that all Joni could see of them was their rapid little legs. Archie stood rigidly, watching them leave. Then he sent a loud whinny after them.

Joni slumped. Archie was an only horse, always hungry for the company of other horses. It would take an enormous amount of hauling rein and thumping ribs to make him move on. Once she got to the far end of North Valley Road, she'd have to turn around and come back and have the fight all over again. Groan-a-*mungo*!

It wasn't feeling like a strong-minded afternoon anymore. Joni turned Archie back toward the white house and the new girl. She might as well get this over with!

THREE

Captive Animals

At the white house, a small table and two folding chairs were set out at the bottom of the lawn. The new—no. *Chess*. Her name was Chess, and she was walking carefully down the lawn, carrying a tray with a large sweating pitcher, two glasses, and several carrots.

She put the tray on the table. "My mom thought you might be thirsty. Do you want to get off?"

Joni didn't. She wanted to cross the bridge and go down the quieter branch of the road, where she was guaranteed not to meet anyone. But she couldn't say that, and anyway, she was thirsty. She dismounted and loosened the cinch. Archie shook himself, rattling the saddle loudly.

"Can I give him a carrot?" Chess asked.

"Okay." Archie smelled the carrots already, and Joni was having a hard time holding him back.

Chess held a carrot out on the flat of her hand, with her fingers stretched back out of the way. So she knew how to feed a horse, or she'd read about it. Joni saw her flinch as Archie fumbled with his lips. The carrot rolled off, and he dived for it. It disappeared in two juicy bites.

"Here," Joni said. "Like this." She took another carrot and stood it on its fat end in the palm of her hand, holding it steady with her fingers. She put it under Archie's quivering silver lips. It disappeared inside his head as Joni pushed it upward.

Chess laughed. "Like a food processor!"

The laugh did it—a deep, rich, adult-sounding chuckle, a little like Archie's nicker, a laugh that said Chess totally got how great it was to feed a carrot to a horse. She grabbed a third carrot from the table and fed it to Archie the food processor way. Joni laughed and reached for the fourth, then paused.

"No, that's a lot. He could get—"

Archie snatched the carrot. "Okay!" Joni said. "I guess four won't hurt him—no, Archie, they're gone. Eat grass!"

"Hurt him?" Chess asked. She looked worried.

"He'll be fine," Joni said. You had to be careful about overfeeding horses, but four carrots wasn't that much, and anyway, it was too late.

Chess seemed to have forgotten the lemonade. Holding the reins, Joni sat on one of the chairs and poured herself a glass. It was the homemade, sour, puckery kind.

"Oh," Chess said. "Sorry." She and Joni looked at each other, and they both laughed again.

13

"Where do you live?" Chess asked. "I didn't see a house from the bus stop."

Joni explained, drawing a map on the table with lemonade so Chess understood how the farm road, the big field, and the trail beside the brook connected with North Valley Road. "It's a lot closer that way than it is by the main road."

"But you ride through the woods?"

Joni nodded. She was about to say that the woods were easy, it was nothing, nobody could possibly get lost on that trail, but Chess looked impressed, so she decided not to.

"You're from California? Why did you guys move here?" She'd wondered about that with Danae and Alyssa.

"My dad got a job here." Chess folded her lips, like there was more she wasn't saying.

"Didn't your parents care that you'd have to leave your school?"

"School was almost over, anyway. My grandmother moved back to her own apartment, and Mom didn't want to take care of us all by herself, so we came with Dad instead of waiting. I have a little brother," she explained. "He was born too early, so he gets sick a lot. And you live on a farm, right? 'Cause there's a farm sign at your bus stop."

Joni explained that Dad raised sheep, and milked them, and made sheep's milk cheese that won awards. "He's won, like, the Academy Award of cheese," she said, hoping for another of those laughs. Chess did laugh, but it wasn't an Archie-eating-carrots-level laugh, just a quick chuckle, and then a question.

"Do the sheep *like* being milked?"

Joni thought of the mad stampede down the milking

platform. Each sheep shoved her nose into her grain bucket. Then Dad pulled a lever that closed two bars of metal around each neck. The sheep were too busy gobbling to notice or care that they were confined, and they hardly paid attention while they were milked. They might kick at the milking machine the first few times, but they got over that.

"They don't *mind*," she said.

"I'm a vegan," Chess said. "So I guess I won't be tasting your dad's cheese."

"A vegan's like a vegetarian, right?"

Chess said, "I don't eat anything that comes from an animal."

"Oh," Joni said. "We grow veggies, too." It sounded lame.

"So listen," Chess said. "That old lady down the road, with the ponies?"

"Actually, they're miniature horses," Joni said.

"Whatever!" Chess's eyes glittered—with tears, Joni realized. Her eyes were actually full of tears! "They need to be rescued!"

Joni felt her mouth hang open. *Rescue?* The minis were round and fat, but not too fat. They had a shady paddock and a barn, and an owner who loved them. Or at least, an owner who knew exactly how to manage them. Joni's 4-H group volunteered at Kalysta's Kritters, the local horse shelter, every other Sunday. She'd met lots of horses who'd been rescued, and they were so not Mrs. Abernathy's minis!

"She keeps them in that tiny little pen!" Chess said. "They're surrounded by gorgeous green grass, but she hardly ever lets them out. And when she *does* let them out, she makes them wear muzzles! How can they even *eat*?"

"Those are probably—"

"*And* she makes them drag her around all the time, and she's *huge!*"

"Yeah, but—"

"But what bothers me the most," Chess said, "is they never have a second when they aren't wearing a restraint!"

"You mean, a *halter?*" A restraint was something that controlled a horse, like Archie's hackamore, with its strong noseband and metal cheek pieces. But a halter was only a restraint when someone was holding it, or the horse was tied. Otherwise, it was like clothes, like a hat. "That's not—"

"When you see something like that, you have to *do* something," Chess said. Her eyes were bright and her cheeks flushed. "They're being abused, and we have to rescue them!"

We? How did it get to be we *so fast?* "It's bad for horses to eat too much," Joni said. "They get sick. At Kalysta's, there's this horse—"

"Excuse me, *grass?*" Chess said. "Grass is natural! They *evolved* to eat grass!"

Joni stared helplessly. Yes, horses evolved to eat grass, but wild grass, Ice Age grass, not lush Vermont hayfields. *So say that!* Why couldn't she be a better talker? Chess didn't know a thing about horses, but how could Joni make her understand when she couldn't even finish a sentence?

"Do you have any pets?" she asked, because a change of subject would be great right now.

Chess shook her head. "We don't believe in keeping captive animals."

We aren't going to be friends, Joni thought. How many

captive animals did her family have? Three hundred sheep and lambs, four dogs, a cat and kittens, Archie . . .

"I should get going." She stood up and tried to tighten the cinch. Archie swelled up against it, and Joni walked him around until he let his breath out.

"'Bye." She put her foot in the stirrup and grabbed the saddle horn to pull herself up. Instantly, the saddle slipped, and dumped her flat on her back.

"Are you okay?" Chess was bending over her.

"No, I'm stupid!" Joni felt much better all of a sudden. Everything looked different from here. The trees were upside down. Archie's belly was big and round, and the saddle was on his side, not his back. Chess looked different, too, a little worried, a little confused. There was no point in being shy anymore. Joni had nothing left to lose.

"He fills his belly up with air so I can't tighten the cinch," she said. "I walked him around so he'd have to breathe, but then I forgot to do up the cinch."

"I guess he doesn't like it tight," Chess said.

"Tough! I don't like falling off!" Joni got up. Archie stood, looking smug. He didn't bother to bloat again. He'd made his point. Joni yarned the cinch up tight. "Can I stand on your chair to mount?" It was the gray metal cafeteria kind, nice and sturdy.

"Sure," Chess said. Joni mounted and turned Archie toward the bridge.

"See you tomorrow morning," Chess called. "On the bus."

On the bus. Would Chess expect Joni to sit with her? What about when Danae and Alyssa got on? Always, Joni saved them seat number eleven. There were only two more days to do that, ever. Next year, they'd be the youngest kids riding on the high school bus . . .

Archie was trotting. Not good. On the way home, that tended to turn into a stampede. "Just walk," Joni said, putting pressure on the reins. Archie obeyed, but it was a quick walk that kept bubbling over into a trot the second she stopped paying attention.

Was he a captive? Did he hate his life? Joni looked at his perky white ears. No, that was ridiculous. Sure, he'd be happier if he got unlimited grass—and he'd eat himself sick, so that was never going to happen! And, yes, he'd probably like another horse to live with. And maybe he'd rather win every tussle with Joni—or maybe he'd get bored, like Joni would if he suddenly stopped trying to get his own way.

They came out into the field. From here, the farm looked like a toy, set down in the middle of the surrounding woods. The tiny barn was brilliant red. Dark green maple trees lined the edges of the pastures. The hillside was dotted with cottony white sheep . . .

No, with captive animals.

"Oh, I don't care!" Joni said. "Trot!"

FOUR

"Get Off and Walk!"

Luckily, Dad was busy milking, because it was a bit of a mad stampede back to the barn. Joni took care of Archie, then raced up to the hayloft for a hasty look at the kittens she was civilizing. All there. All sleeping. Instead of cuddling them, she rushed indoors to call Danae. Alyssa would be there, too. She stayed at Danae's house after school, till her mother got home.

"So, the new girl," Joni said. "I talked with her. She lives in the white house on North Valley Road."

"And *she* talked to *you*?" Danae asked.

"Yes. She's . . . nice." That wasn't the right word. Chess was interesting. And alarming. "Anyway, we talked," Joni said.

"Cool!" Alyssa said. "Ask her to sit with us tomorrow."

So when Joni got on the bus the next morning, and Chess

looked up from her seat behind the driver, Joni said, "Come on," and led the way back to seat eleven. Seat ten was empty, too. All the seats were empty. Joni had always been the last kid on the bus at night, and the first kid on in the morning, before Chess.

"How's Archie?" Chess asked.

"He's okay," Joni said. She'd seen him from a distance, grazing in his small, eaten-down pasture. He had the brook to drink from, so he could take care of himself till she got home. "That's one of Dad's fields," Joni said, pointing out the window. "And he hays the one on the other side of the road, too, but that doesn't belong to us."

"What do you mean, 'hays'?" Chess asked. "Like, *hey*?" She waved her hand in a cool, possibly California way.

"No, he makes hay." Did Chess even know what hay was? "It's dried grass," she said. "It's what the animals eat in the winter." But here they were talking about animals again. Joni had hoped to avoid that.

"Do you ride Archie up here?" Chess asked.

"I'm not allowed to take him on the main road," Joni said. "Too many cars. But I ride through the fields to Danae's house, if Dad doesn't have the sheep fence in the way." Chess didn't understand that, either. Joni explained about the electric fences that Dad moved from field to field to give the sheep fresh grass. Sometimes she could find a way around them. Sometimes she had to give up and go home. It was up to her to get there because Danae's pony, Pumpkin, was afraid of the Bears. Mom or Dad would drive her up there if she asked, but Joni liked having her own independent way back home, especially in the summer. Danae and Alyssa spent every day together then, and things were different.

What if *she* had a friend next door? What would that be like?

The bus stopped. Danae and Alyssa got on, taking seat ten, and Joni introduced them, because nobody had talked to anybody yesterday.

"So, why did you come to school for just the last three days?" Danae asked.

Chess made a face. "I didn't want to stay home and take care of my little brother!"

"And you're from California?" Alyssa said. "I went there once."

"California's huge," Danae said. "That's like saying, 'I've been to earth'!" Chess laughed, and Joni relaxed. This was easy.

They talked about huge California, and about Vermont, which was so small and green. "And quiet!" Chess said. "How do you sleep at night?" Which made them laugh, but she wasn't joking.

"I guess I'll just get used to it," she said. "Where's the nearest place to get falafel?"

"What's falafel?" Joni asked.

"My grandmother and I go out for it all the time," Chess said. "Used to go out for it. It's chickpeas, all fried up crunchy and garlicky and salty, on pita bread, with this sauce—"

"It's kind of like a burger," Alyssa explained. Chess didn't hear because Danae was telling her where to get falafel—not nearby, unfortunately.

"There was a place right down at the end of our street," Chess said, and she got that Closed expression.

Joni, Danae, and Alyssa all looked at one another. Danae said, "We go sometimes. Next time, I'll ask if you can come, too."

"Thanks," Chess said. But it wasn't about the falafel, Joni could tell.

At school, it was cleanup day. They gathered books from desks and other odd places, and helped Mrs. Emmons put them away. "So, what do you like to read?" Alyssa asked Chess.

"Rescue stories."

"Rescuing what?" Danae asked.

"Animals. All kinds of animals." Joni felt a pulse of worry in her stomach.

"Did you ever read *The Incredible Journey*?" Danae said. "It's this really cool story about two dogs and a cat that rescue themselves."

"The movie's fantastic!" Alyssa said. "When they get back with their people, I cry, every time."

Chess didn't say anything. She was probably thinking, *Silly animals! Putting themselves back in captivity.* Joni did *not* want to go down that rabbit hole.

"Do you like the Cinderella movie?" she asked. It felt really obvious. She wasn't good at clever moves like changing the subject.

But it turned out to be a brilliant question. The other three each liked a different Cinderella movie, and the debate lasted through school and on the bus ride, all the way to Danae and Alyssa's bus stop.

Now only Joni and Chess were left on the bus. Silence fell. It had been a long day, fun and sociable, so Joni needed her ride on Archie. Alone. It was important, like Mom's coffee in the morning, or Dad's weird buttermilk drink during haying season.

But what did Chess expect? Nothing was said until Joni stood up to get off the bus.

"See you later?" Chess asked.

Joni opened her mouth to say no. Instead, she said, "Uh—sure."

She biked slowly down the farm road, mad at herself. Why had she said that? Because she was nice—wimpy nice. Now she was stuck.

She could just not go. She could say Archie had misbehaved, or that she'd forgotten a doctor's appointment. But Chess wouldn't believe her. Nobody believed Joni when she lied. She walked into the house, and Dad handed her the phone. "Your sister," he said.

"Hey!" It was Olivia. "I'm coming home!"

"You *are*? When?"

"Who knows!" Olivia said happily. "We're on our bicycles, and visiting friends along the way. It could be a week."

"Are you coming to stay?"

"Yes. We just quit our jobs. Remember Rosita, from my graduation? Daddy doesn't have an intern this summer, so we're going to make cheese and help him hay. Then—who knows? Grad school, maybe? Or I could go into the Peace Corps. Hey, I can't *wait* to see you, Jon-Jon!"

"Me, either!" Joni said. Olivia was her favorite sister. Kate

23

always knew best, but Olivia listened, and stayed up late with Joni, talking about things. "Do you *have* to bike?" Joni asked. "Couldn't Dad go get you?"

Olivia laughed. "Daddy's got one or two other things to do! Hang in there, kiddo. I'm in New York State. I'll be there in no time. Let me talk to him again, okay?"

Joni handed Dad the phone, feeling a lot better. Olivia would understand about the captive animal thing. If there was a problem, she would help Joni smooth things out. Or maybe it wouldn't matter anymore. Because with Olivia home all summer, Joni wouldn't need a friend next door. She'd have one right here.

Chess waited at the bottom of the lawn again. This time she was leaning on a bike. "Mom says I can ride along with you, if that's okay."

"*Horse!*" A little boy stood on the lawn, holding a slender woman's hand. He waved. "*Horse!*" Joni waved back, even though she knew he was waving at Archie.

"*Is* it okay?" Chess asked. "Will the bike scare him?"

Once again, there was a way out, and once again, Joni found herself not taking it. "Nothing scares Archie." Other than the llama that time, and who could blame him? Llamas kind of looked like space aliens.

They headed down the road. Chess labored over the pedals, not like Olivia, flying along like a bird somewhere out in western New York. Whenever she managed a burst of speed, Archie quickened his pace to stay ahead. Chess was too breathless to talk.

At Mrs. Abernathy's driveway she slowed, coasting down the middle of the road with her head turned toward the house and barn. Archie looked, too, but there was no sign of the minis or their owner. Good! This was all easier than Joni had expected—and quieter.

They reached the intersection with the main road as a river of brown cows crossed it. Somebody stood in the road on each side of the herd, but the cows needed no guidance. They knew where they were going and had their minds on supper.

Chess said, "I thought cows were black and white."

"These are Jerseys," Joni said, trying not to sound superior. She and Danae had asked some questions about California today that were probably just as dumb, and Chess had been nice about it. "They give less milk than the black-and-white cows, but it has more cream. Dad uses some of these cows' milk to make cheese."

Chess probably thought milk was gross. But she didn't say anything, just stood watching the cows. Then she looked over her shoulder. "I'm surprised my mom isn't coming to check up on me already! Your parents let you go anywhere?"

"Anywhere" was this dirt road, and the back pasture route to Danae's and Alyssa's, and a few trails through the woods. Still—

"Yes," Joni said.

"You're brave." Chess sounded glum, and Joni didn't know what to say. She was brave. She was on Archie! Other than him, there wasn't much to be brave about around here.

"I'd be really chicken in a city," she said.

"No, you wouldn't," Chess said. "After a week, you'd be totally used to it."

"Well. How long have you been here?" Joni asked.

Chess looked startled. After a second, she laughed, that adult-sounding chuckle. "Four days. No, five. Okay, I get it! And I'm not scared. I just don't know my way around. And my mom keeps—hovering!"

Joni made a sympathetic noise. Mom and Dad didn't believe in hovering over kids—though if they'd heard some of the stories Kate and Olivia told about their free-range adventures, they might think differently. But there were two Big Girls. There was only one of Joni, and she was a lot more careful.

The last cow disappeared into the barn. Joni and Chess turned toward home. "Okay," Chess said. "Which of these plants is poison ivy?"

"There isn't poison ivy on this road," Joni said. "There's a patch along the edge of our field. I'll show you what it looks like."

"And are there bears?"

Joni laughed. "Yes."

"What's funny?" Chess asked.

"Slow down, Archie!" Joni said. Now she wanted to talk. "Out in the woods there's black bears, and on the farm we have polar bears!"

No reaction. She looked down at Chess, who had stopped paying attention. They were passing Mrs. Abernathy's driveway, and she had her head turned, looking out across the fields. Still no minis—

No, here they came out of the woods, Mrs. Abernathy seated like a gigantic statue on the cart. A slender log dragged on the ground behind it, the front end raised up a few inches.

Good idea, Joni thought. That way, the log couldn't stub into a rock or—

Chess brought the bike to a swerving stop. "Poor babies! Dragging a cart *and* a log *and* that huge fat woman?"

She cupped her hands to her mouth like a megaphone.

"*Hey!* Why don't you get off and *walk!*"

FIVE

Character

Joni's mouth fell open. She looked down at Chess, and then out across the field, where Mrs. Abernathy was turning her head. Looking at them.

It wasn't me! Joni clapped her heels to Archie's sides. His ears swiveled. Was she telling him to run? She never let him run on the road, especially on the way home.

Joni kicked him again. He took off at a rattling gallop that loosened her in the saddle and whipped tears into her eyes. She grabbed for his mane. Steady, better, but with her hands full of mane, she couldn't pull on the reins and now Archie was running away with her.

"Whoa!" Joni yelled. "Whoa!" He flicked one ear at her and poured on the speed, aiming himself down the road like a silver spear. He would swerve at the rocks, and jump over them, and she would fall off.

Joni clamped her jaw. "You are going to *stop*!" She let go of his mane and seized the left rein in both hands. With all her might, she hauled his head toward Chess's driveway. She felt herself slip in the saddle, but her grip on the rein kept her from falling. Archie thundered up the driveway, and the little boy came running straight toward them.

Archie dug in his front feet and stopped abruptly. Joni slammed into his neck. She wrapped her arms around it, and managed to keep from diving off over his shoulder. As she straightened, she saw a spatter of blood in his white mane.

Her blood.

"Horse!" the boy said.

Joni pressed the back of her hand against her lip, staring down at him. He was little and thin, like Chess, with pale skin and a wide smile. He reached his hands to Archie. Joni looked up to meet his mother's wide eyes.

She couldn't think of a thing to say.

Chess skidded the bicycle to a halt beside her. "Wow, he's so fast!"

Their mother picked up the little boy and opened her mouth. No words came out.

"Yes," Joni said. "He's . . . he is fast." She looked at the splotch of blood on her hand and touched her tongue to her lip. It felt sort of mashed, and tasted salty, but nothing was trickling down her chin.

Archie stretched his nose toward the little boy. He loved small children. He scrubbed his silver, whiskery upper lip on the boy's hair, producing squeals and giggles. But all Joni could think of were the long metal shanks of the hackamore. If Archie moved his head wrong . . .

The mother stepped back, taking the boy out of reach. Joni opened her mouth.

No. There really was nothing to say.

She turned Archie back down the driveway. Her body felt shaky, but her hands were firm on the reins. Archie pranced, ready for more galloping.

Chess coasted beside them. "Wow! How do you dare go that fast?"

Did she not know that Archie had almost run over her little brother? "Why did you *yell* at—ow!" Joni dabbed her lip. It was still bleeding.

"Because it's *abuse!*" Chess said.

"No, it isn't!"

"They shouldn't be forced to drag a huge load like that!" Chess said. "Getting off is the least she could do!"

"But it wasn't huge!" Joni said. "Horses are strong. They can—"

"Just because they *can* doesn't mean they *should!*" Chess's cheeks were bright, and her eyes shone. "Animals shouldn't be slaves. They deserve better than that!"

But this was so crazy! Here Joni was sitting on top of Archie, her slave. Why wasn't Chess yelling at her? "She's an *old lady!*"

Chess lifted her chin. "My grandmother says an activist comforts the afflicted, and afflicts the comfortable."

"Well, *I* don't!" Joni loosened the reins and let Archie have his head. He shot forward, clattered across the bridge, and leaped over the big rocks. It was an enormous jump, and Joni rode it pretty well considering that she'd never jumped anything that big before. She let him canter almost all the way down the trail. But the canter was turning into a gallop, and the next stage after that was runaway.

"Walk, Archie—ow!" She licked her lip. Was that going to show? This was an afternoon she *really* didn't want to talk about! She fought him to a walk, then a standstill, and let him eat some maple leaves while he caught his breath. He still jigged when they came out into the open, though. Joni managed to control him by zigzagging along the edge of the field, never letting him gain momentum.

She spotted the patch of poison ivy, its leaves slick and oily-looking. She would point that out to Chess—

No, she probably wouldn't. They probably weren't going to be friends. How could Joni hang out with somebody who would behave that way to an old person? Even thinking about it made her feel hot all over.

In the farmyard, the border collies crouched, watching the door of the milking parlor. Any second now it would open and let out a batch of sheep, sheep that needed bossing. Any second! The dogs spared quick glances at Joni, flattening their ears. Hi. We're busy.

She led Archie into the cool stall, took off his saddle and bridle, and rubbed him down with his own private towel. He ducked his head into her hands, pushing hard. He loved having his face wiped.

She got him two carrots from his bag, stashed in a cool crevice in the rock foundation. Archie nickered. It was one of

Joni's favorite sounds in the whole world. Now it reminded her of Chess's laugh. *Oh, groan!* This was the kind of complicated feeling a ride was supposed to take away.

She let Archie out. He rolled in the dirt, his four legs waving in the air. Then he stood up, shook in a cloud of dust, and wandered off, inspecting the grass to see if it had grown at all in the hour he'd been gone. His pasture was very small, and the grass was short—all for good reason, but Joni knew what Chess would say.

She went to peek at herself in the milk house mirror. Her lower lip was fatter than normal, but not horrible. Maybe no one would notice.

She found Mom and Dad at the back end of a row of sheep. The sheep stood on the waist-high metal platform, and Dad was attaching a milking machine to the last one's udder. Mom put an arm around Joni's shoulders. "How was your day, sweetie?"

Joni ducked her head into Mom's side. Archie almost killed a little kid and Chess yelled at Mrs. Abernathy. Other than that . . . no. She couldn't talk about it.

Luckily, there was Olivia's call to discuss. Dad was delighted that she was coming, and not just because she was Olivia. He didn't have any farm interns lined up for this summer, and he needed the help. "She wants the barn apartment," he told Mom. "And she's bringing a friend!"

"Girl or boy?" Mom asked.

"It's Rosita," Dad said. "Remember her?

"Okay," Mom said. "Joni, have you done your kittens today?"

"Not yet." Obviously, Mom wanted to talk to Dad without

her around. She climbed the stairs to the hayloft. The afternoon sun flooded through the wide door, lighting the vast space. High above, in the shadowy rafters, swallows swooped back and forth from their nests.

The mother cat rushed to greet Joni, with a loud meow, ignoring the swallows that dive-bombed her. She stared straight into Joni's eyes, urgent and commanding. Then she turned and headed toward the back of the haymow, looking over her shoulder to be sure Joni was following.

"Did you move them again? Where—oh, I see."

In a cave between the bales, the four young kittens bumbled over one another. Their mother crawled in and curled her body around them, beaming proudly. It was Joni's job to play with them so they wouldn't grow up wild. Yesterday, she'd only peeked at them because she'd been in a hurry to tell Danae and Alyssa about Chess . . .

She picked up each kitten in turn, kissing them, stroking their tiny heads. They looked at her with milky blue, bewildered eyes, and opened their pink mouths in squeaking cries.

"It's okay," Joni crooned. "Good babies. You're going to love people." Soon they would start to purr, and then to play. Then they'd be easy to give away—

"Oh! Maybe Chess—"

No. Chess wouldn't want a captive animal.

"How could anybody not want you?" Joni cradled the last kitten against her cheek. He was as soft as a pussy willow, and shaking with—

No, he wasn't shaking! He was *purring*! Joni stroked her

cheek against him. "You're so brave!" she whispered. She was a giant to him, a giant of another species. But he put forth this amazing, happy sound and hooked her. She would do anything for him.

She kissed him, and looked down into his mother's large green eyes. She seemed satisfied, as if she had planned this all along—and maybe she had. Even before the kittens were born, she'd taken Joni and Dad and anyone else who would follow to see her secret nest. She wanted them to know and love her kittens, and why? It was the best thing for the kittens, but how could a cat know that?

Joni kissed the kitten, nestled him back beside his mother, and filled up the food dish. Then she ran down to the milking parlor—interrupting what they were saying, but this was important.

"One's purring! The gray one with the white bib!"

"That's great, Joni!" Dad said. He'd let a new batch of sheep in, and he was wiping down their freckled udders while they gobbled.

"What did you do to your lip?" Mom asked.

"Oh, Archie stopped fast."

"And you didn't!" Mom said. "If ponies build character, I'd say you've got character out to here, kiddo!"

Joni's spirits took a little dip. Compared with Chess, she didn't have character at all. Okay, she was brave enough to ride a horse like Archie, but she could never yell at an old lady, especially one like Mrs. Abernathy. She didn't want to, but she would like to know that she *dared* to. Or maybe not yell, but at least speak up. That had never been a problem for Kate and Olivia, as far as she could see, and Danae and Alyssa were great speaker-uppers, but Joni didn't fight with people. "My happy camper," Dad sometimes called her.

A happy camper and an activist did not seem like a great match.

"I'll go check on supper," Mom said. Joni remembered the smell of lamb stew from the slow cooker. Oh! And she remembered Mrs. Abernathy's message from yesterday.

"Dad, that lady on North Valley Road, the one with the miniature horses? She said to tell you she wants two lambs."

"How is she?" Mom asked. "When did you see her?"

"Um—yesterday. I forgot to tell you last night."

"And how was she?" Mom repeated.

Joni shrugged. How was she supposed to know how Mrs. Abernathy was, when she didn't even know the lady? But Mom was a writer and a high school writing teacher. She was always trying to get people—mostly Dad and Joni—to pay attention to details. Joni groped for some details she could tell.

"She was out in her garden. Hilling potatoes, I think. She had her horses and cart."

"Was she alone?" Dad asked.

"No, she had her horses!"

Dad laughed. "I meant people. Whenever I go by, there's some man in her yard, cutting wood or fixing something. All the old bachelors and widowers around here are in love with her!"

"Her husband died last fall," Mom explained. "He was sick

for a long time, and she nursed him. That's why nobody knows her very well. They moved in a couple of years ago when he was already sick."

"She was bringing in a log today, with her minis." Joni felt her face burn. She *so* didn't want to think about that scene!

"She used to drive horses in competitions," Mom said. "She had to sell them when her husband got sick. I'm glad she's got those ponies. It's about time life got easier for her."

SIX

"It's O-o-o-o-o-ver!"

On Wednesday, Joni asked Mom to drop her off at school. It was the last day. And she had half a wheel of cheese to take in for the class picnic lunch. Those seemed like good reasons not to ride the bus, but the school year was ending for Mom, too, and she had about a hundred and fifty extra things to do. Dad, of course, was cleaning up after milking.

So Joni got on the bus with her picnic basket and made the long walk down the aisle to seat eleven. Would Chess be mad? Because Joni had ridden away from her. That was like hanging up in the middle of a phone conversation. *She* would be mad! And did that even matter? She'd already decided they weren't going to be friends.

But Chess didn't look mad. "Good!" she said. "You got home okay."

"Why not?"

"He kept running away with you. I was worried. I started to bike after you, but I couldn't keep up."

Unbelievable! Chess didn't know a thing! She hadn't even noticed Joni kicking Archie in the ribs. Joni could say whatever she wanted, about him, or the farm, or animals, and Chess would believe her.

It also meant that Chess didn't think anything was wrong between them. It was up to Joni to let her know. Or not.

"Yeah, I got him under control," she said.

"So," Chess said. "What are we going to do about those ponies?"

"Nothing," Joni said. "It doesn't hurt them to—"

"But that was a huge load they were pulling!"

"They're *strong*!" Joni said, loudly enough that the bus driver looked at her in his mirror. "Ponies are like jeeps—"

"No, they're not," Chess said. "A jeep is a machine. Ponies have *feelings*, they're sensitive—"

"Have you ever *met* a pony?" Joni's heart was pounding. The bus driver looked at her again, and no wonder. This was practically an argument, and Joni had always been the quietest kid on the bus. But it felt surprisingly good when those words blasted out without her even thinking about them. She *could* argue! Maybe she could even win.

Chess didn't answer, because the bus stopped again and Danae and Alyssa came down the aisle—"The last time *ever*!" Alyssa wailed—and suddenly it was all about the three of them.

It was like that in school, too—a day for old friends, not

new. A few people got teary-eyed. "It's over," Alyssa kept saying. "We'll never be sixth graders again."

It was true. For this whole year, they'd been the oldest kids in school, the coolest, and the smartest. Next year, they'd be the youngest in a big district high school. They'd have to start at the bottom again.

So it was a day to remember past triumphs. They explained the old jokes to Chess, and told the old stories—the time Skyler swung so high he went all the way over the top bar of the swing set, the time a teacher fainted in front of the class, the annual class field trip to Joni's farm to see the new lambs . . .

"Remember the year Ray touched the electric fence three times?"

"Remember when Celia stepped in sheep manure?"

"Remember the kindergarten visit? We thought the Polar Bears really *were* bears!"

Chess looked at Joni. "What *are* they, then?" Everybody jumped in to explain. Danae, who could be very loud for a very long time if necessary, talked over all of them. She made it clear that the Bears were big, white, fluffy dogs who lived out in the pasture with the sheep—at least, they were supposed to. They guarded against coyotes and whatever else out there might like a lamb dinner. They were strong fighters, but mostly what they did was bark.

"But they like people better than sheep," Danae said. "So they're around the house a lot, and sometimes sheep get munched."

Not an accurate word for it. Joni hated the sight of wool

pulled across the grass. She tried never to go closer so she wouldn't see the blood and all the rest of it. She didn't want to think about that now.

"We have kittens," she said.

She was getting good at changing the subject. Everyone clamored, "Oh, can I have one?" "Can I?"

"They're too young right now," Joni said, and several people asked if they could come over and see the kittens. Not Chess, though.

But there were other things to talk about besides Joni's farm, and a few actual school-related things to do, and then the potluck picnic. Joni wasn't allowed to cut the big cheese. She was good with a knife. Mom and Dad had taught her carefully. But Mrs. Emmons said, "If they want to let you, that's their business. I'm not having our last day spoiled by you cutting a finger off. Some people are vegetarians, you know!"

"I'm a vegan," Chess said. "I don't eat *anything* that comes from an animal!"

Some people thought they knew what *vegan* meant, but nobody had it exactly right, so Joni learned the range of things that Chess would not eat. Eggs. Milk. Cheese. Ice cream. Of course, no bacon or burgers. Pizza? Only with vegetable toppings and fake cheese. Cake and cookies? Only if made without milk, cream, eggs, or butter. "No wonder you're so skinny," Danae said.

Still, the chocolate cake Chess brought for the picnic was amazing, even better than Mom's. And Chess *could* eat potato chips. That was major.

After lunch, they cleaned out their desks, took down their art projects, and rode the bus home, "for the last time *ever*." Joni got ready for graduation and ate an early supper with Mom and Grandma DeeDee. Dad hurried to finish milking, and they all went back to school.

The gym was loud and crowded, especially around Grandma DeeDee. She'd been the principal until she retired a couple of years ago. Now she was the president of the school board, and busier than ever. Everyone wanted to talk school with her. Joni drifted away to hang out with her class.

People hugged each other (girls) or scuffled (some of the boys), and Alyssa said quite a few times, "It's really over." Chess was there, too, which was a surprise. She'd only been in their class for three days, but the school had decided to include her.

Mrs. Emmons organized the sixth grade up front. There was a short speech from the principal, and an even shorter one from Grandma DeeDee. Joni had laid down the law at supper. Grandma DeeDee was not allowed to mention Joni's name or call attention to her. But could Grandma DeeDee be trusted? She wasn't the most obedient person in the world.

"Sixth grade, you are a great class," Grandma DeeDee started. "People may think you're only children, but I've found that who you are in sixth grade is who you are. Period." She glanced toward Joni and her eyes narrowed in a quick, warm smile, too brief to be embarrassing.

"What you care about now," Grandma DeeDee went on, "you will always care about. You have important things left to learn, and plenty of growing left to do, but when you're grown up and think back to this year, you'll find that it's a touchstone. The sixth grader you are now points the way to the adult you'll someday be."

For a moment, Joni felt comfortable, steady. Great, she didn't have to turn into somebody else.

But, who you are . . . is who you are? So she was always going to be a happy camper, a free-range farm girl? Did she want that? She loved her life, obviously, but at some point, you had to kick things up a notch, like Carleen said. Which meant learning and growing—two easy words that usually involved doing something hard and scary . . .

. . . and maybe Grandma DeeDee went on to say something about that, but Joni suddenly discovered she'd missed that part of the speech. The sixth grade went up one by one to get their diplomas. There was punch and cake—probably not vegan— and then it really *was* over.

Joni walked out the big front doors with Mom and Dad, feeling loose and dislocated. She didn't belong in this school anymore, but she didn't belong in middle school yet, either. Danae and Alyssa were ahead of her in the crowd, Alyssa whispering in Danae's ear. It was starting already, the summer pattern of them spending every day together, except for the week Danae spent with Joni at riding camp . . .

"Horse!"

Chess and her family were right behind them, the little boy riding his father's shoulders. He pointed at Joni. "Horse!" Everybody turned around, even Grandma DeeDee.

"Her name is Joni," Chess said. "His name is Noah."

The parents introduced themselves. They were the Venturas.

"Very glad to meet a friend of Francesca's," Mr. Ventura said.

"Chess," Chess said, under her breath.

Mrs. Ventura still seemed alarmed when she looked at Joni. She must be remembering the Archie episode. But Chess's father said, "You're the people with the sheep farm, right? And you actually milk them and make cheese? I'll have to try some of that!" So *he* wasn't a vegan.

"Do either of you plan to join the PTO?" Grandma DeeDee asked Chess's mother. There she went, taking more captives! Joni moved away, embarrassed, and suddenly Chess was beside her.

"Can I come see your kittens?"

"Sure!" Joni was too startled to ask herself whether she wanted Chess to come, until after the word had burst out.

"Tomorrow I can't," Chess said. "Mom's shopping and I have to help with Noah. But I'll call. You guys are in the phone book, right?"

"Yes." They were in the phone book, and also right there at the end of the brook trail, and at the end of the farm road, easily found from any direction. There was no escape. Joni would just have to deal.

She broke away and grabbed Alyssa from behind, tickling her ribs. "It's *over*, Alyssa! It's o-o-o-o-o-ver!"

SEVEN

Mrs. Abernathy

The first day of summer vacation was a day to sleep late. Mom made bacon and French toast, Joni's favorite, for breakfast, and all three of them stayed at the table for a long time, talking. Mom had high school graduation this afternoon, and then her vacation began. Dad's busy season, milking and cheese making and haying, was just getting started. So this was a rare moment of peace for them. When the phone rang, they looked into one another's eyes. Then Dad made a reluctant face and answered it.

"Yes? Oh, yes, I did get that message! Could I pen the dogs?" His eyebrows rose. *Who was asking him to do that?* Joni wondered. "Are they okay with the border collies? Okay. Fine. I'll do that."

Hanging up, he said, "Your friend Mrs. Abernathy, Joni.

She's coming to pay for the lambs, and she wants the Bears penned up."

"She can't be afraid of dogs, can she?" Mom asked.

"The ponies might be. She's driving them over. Can you shut the Bears in their pen, Joni?"

"Okay." Mrs. Abernathy was the last person Joni wanted to see, after what happened on Tuesday. But this was her chance to observe the minis close up. She could judge their weight and fitness, and look into their eyes. If they were as healthy and perky as they looked from a distance, she could tell Chess, "They're fine. They're okay." And if they weren't . . . But they would be. She was almost sure.

The Bears lay wagging on the grass beside the milk house. They lacked people skills like leading or heeling. She had to tug each one along by its collar. She closed them in their chain-link pen and filled their water dish. The Bears flopped down, as if they'd just put in a day's work, and encouraged her to scratch their bellies.

"Sorry," Joni said. "You guys are gross!" The white fur on their bellies was brown and greasy from constant lying in sheep pastures. Tasha, the younger one, moaned and pawed the air. "Later," Joni promised. "I'll put on gloves."

Suddenly, Tasha lurched upright and gave a thunderous bark, staring down the field. Niko stood beside her, looking in the same direction. Then he added his deeper warning. After a moment, the minis came out of the woods, pulling Mrs. Abernathy in the cart.

They turned briskly up the field, their eight little legs twinkling. Mrs. Abernathy looked huge behind them, like some giant float in a parade. They must have gone right past Chess's house. How did *that* go? Maybe the Venturas had gone shopping already. But how did Mrs. Abernathy get the cart around the big rocks? She must be a daring driver!

The minis came on at a rapid trot. Their tiny ears pricked toward the farm buildings, then back at their driver, lively and alert. The chestnut was faster, Joni saw. Mrs. Abernathy kept touching the black one with her whip, just lightly, reminding him to do his share.

Dad came out to the yard and called the border collies. They circled toward him—they never made a straight line if they could make a curved one—and crouched at his feet. Mom came out, too, and Joni joined them as the cart rumbled up the slope into the farmyard. The border collies whined, quivering all over. No wonder! The minis were not much bigger than sheep. They stopped, blowing and puffing, craning their necks to see past the blinders.

"Hello, Ruth!" Dad said.

"Hello, Steve, Melanie. Joni, would you mind standing at their heads? No need to touch the bridles unless they move!"

It was a command, not a suggestion. Joni did as she was told. The minis reached their noses toward her—perfect little inquisitive horse noses, reaching *up*. Their long whiskers trembled. Their dark eyes rolled, looking friendly, mischievous, smart. How could Joni not have liked minis? They were horses. They were tiny. What was not to like?

Mrs. Abernathy got out of the cart. Standing on her own two feet, she wasn't huge after all, just a normal-sized older lady.

"Thanks!" she said to Joni. "Meet Kubota." She pointed to the chestnut mini. "And JD."

"JD!" Dad said. "For John Deere?"

"Yes," Mrs. Abernathy said. "His original name was Muffin—can you believe it? Since they were going to be my garden tractors, I thought they should have proper tractor names."

"I always heard it was bad luck to change an animal's name," Mom said.

"I believe in making your own luck!" Mrs. Abernathy's mouth twisted and she gave a short bark of laughter. "Ha! Look how well that's worked out! But a name is just a cue. It means, 'Hey you!' They're perfectly capable of learning more than one word for that." She reached into the side pocket of her jacket and brought out a check. "I believe this is the amount we agreed on."

Dad looked at the check and nodded. "Do you want me to deliver them, or will you take them in the cart?"

"That might be asking too much of these guys. The bleating, I mean. The weight is nothing." She slanted a quick glance at Joni. "They can pull more than twice their weight. Did you know that?"

A slow wave of heat rolled up Joni's face. *She thinks it was me!* Maybe Mrs. Abernathy didn't even see Chess, down there at bike level. Maybe she heard a shout, saw Joni across the field on Archie—and now Joni was being educated!

"Really?" Dad said. "Twice their weight?"

"Yes," Mrs. Abernathy said. "And that's on a sled, not a wheeled vehicle. This pair has won pulling contests against draft horses."

"*No!*" Mom said.

"Yes. Some pulling contests are judged by the proportion of body weight each team pulls. Ponies have a lower center of gravity, so they're tremendously powerful, and minis are even more so. This team was banned from competition, they won so many times! I don't ask anything like that of them, but they make themselves useful." Joni caught that quick glance again. Her face burned.

"I'm so glad you have them," Mom said. "It must be good to have horses again."

Mrs. Abernathy smiled. It made her square, plain face look suddenly handsome. "I never thought I'd be caught dead driving minis. I had a pair of coal-black Morgans! But I can't afford horses like that anymore, and I can't do justice to them. There are thousands of these little beasts around the country eating their heads off, perfectly useless, so I thought—why not? They're cheap to feed, they work cheerfully—it's better than having a man on the place!"

Dad laughed, and Joni saw him decide against making a comment. "How are your potatoes coming along?" he asked. Good! Potatoes were a nice, safe thing for them to talk about.

She looked the minis over, trying to do a body score the way Kalysta had taught their 4-H group. She'd give these guys a Seven, she decided, or maybe an Eight—Fleshy, or Fat. Their spines made little dents down the centers of their plump backs. She'd have to prod their sides hard to even *find* a rib. On the other hand, they seemed fit. On this warm morning, they were barely sweating, and already their breathing had gone back to normal. They were certainly not being overworked.

That wouldn't be enough for Chess, though. Joni could hear her. *Do they like pulling the cart?*

And who knew? Who could read a horse's heart? The eyes behind the blinders looked calm, cheerful, curious. Their focus had shifted to the grass that grew thick and lush at the edge of the dirt road, just like Archie's would. They wanted some, but they didn't need it. If he was happy, they were happy.

She put her hands down to their faces. Two small muzzles poked into her palms, not nipping, just checking. Was it possible that she had treats? Kubota's muzzle quivered. In the middle of saying something to Dad, Mrs. Abernathy made one of those noises. "Uh!" Kubota went still, his eyes widening innocently. Joni wanted to kiss his little nose, but she wasn't sure Mrs. Abernathy would go for that.

"I should let you people get back to work," Mrs. Abernathy said at last. "Will you head them again, Joni?" She got into the cart, settled herself, gathered the reins, and took up the whip, all in the same methodical way Joni had seen before. It was pretty much exactly the opposite of how Joni rode, but it was cool, the way they stood and waited, the way Mrs. Abernathy took time for every detail.

She nodded. Joni stepped away from the minis. Mrs. Abernathy spoke to them, and they leaned into the collars, starting the cart with a little jerk. They made a wide circle in the farmyard and headed back down across the field.

"Whew!" Dad said. "I guess she's doing okay!"

Mom said, "I'm sure she feels more than she says."

49

EIGHT

Eyes

Chess called that night after supper. "I can come tomorrow morning, if you meet me."

"Meet you where?" Joni asked.

"At the bridge," Chess said. "My parents are afraid I'll get lost."

Nobody could get lost on that trail! But the Venturas didn't know that. "Okay, what time?"

"Eight thirty."

Eight thirty? It was summer! It was time to not have any plans, let alone eight-thirty-in-the-morning plans. "Nine," Joni said.

She was ready at eight thirty, anyway. She'd forgotten what

summer was like. Quiet. Really quiet. After a day at school, Joni loved that quiet, and the freedom opening up around her. But on a summer morning with Mom sleeping late and Dad busy in the barn, freedom seemed more like boredom. Danae and Alyssa were probably doing something together already. Joni wished she lived closer to them.

Well, she did live close to Chess. She trotted Archie across the field and down the brook trail, wondering. Could this work? If they avoided Mrs. Abernathy? Because—that laugh. And the way Chess asked questions and spoke her mind. She seemed more grown up than Joni felt, but Chess actually admired *her*. Thought she was brave.

Anyway, how amazing was it that there were any kids at the white house, let alone a girl Joni's age! It was meant to be.

They came upon a line of miniature horse poop. "Cute!" Joni said. Archie put his nose down to sniff it. Then he sniffed along the whole rest of the trail, just like a dog. It had been twenty-four hours since the minis came this way, but he could still smell them—

"Hi!"

Archie jolted to a stop, throwing his head up. Chess sat on one of the big rocks at the end of the trail. Her bike leaned up against it.

Archie blew his breath out loudly. Joni could feel his whole body surging backward. "Say something!" she yelled. "He doesn't know what you are!"

"Oh. Sorry. *Why* doesn't he know?" Chess slid off the rock, and Archie's neck softened. Now he could see that this was a person he knew, and not a talking rock.

"Horses don't see like we do," Joni said. "They have a hard time focusing on things in front of them."

"But they can see all around themselves, right?" Chess asked. "I read that."

"Sort of," Joni said. "Their eyes are on the sides of their heads, so they see out to the sides. But it's like—well, put your hands up beside your ears."

Chess obeyed. "I can sort of see them."

"But you can't count your fingers, right?" Joni said. "Not without turning your head. That's what it's like for them. They can see a lot, but it's pretty out of focus."

Chess stood with her hands up, slowly wiggling her fingers. "Wow," she said. "How can they run if they see that badly?"

"I don't know."

"But you ride him!" Chess said. "It's like, if my dad smeared hand cream all over his windshield and then drove seventy miles an hour. I mean—you go *fast*! How do you *dare*?"

"I don't think about it," Joni said. This was embarrassing. The last time she'd ridden Archie fast, she was running away from Chess. "Let's go." She turned Archie back toward the farm. Chess followed on her bike. The trail was flat and fairly smooth, but Chess bumped and puffed, and dropped behind.

"It's easier to walk," Joni called. "Leave your bike here."

"I didn't bring my lock."

"Nobody will take it. There isn't anybody!"

But Chess wheeled the bike all the way to the field, and left it leaning against a tree. She walked along beside Archie. "I've been thinking about those poor ponies."

"Miniature horses. They're fine!" Joni said. "She drove them here yesterday and I saw them up close. They're in great shape! Did you know that ponies can pull—"

"But their *eyes*!" Chess said. "Imagine if you could see the way they do! Three hundred and sixty degrees! And then they have to wear those blinders and they can't see any of it! Just that little bit in front of them."

"But that's because—" Because why? Actually, Joni always felt a little sad when she saw driving horses wearing blinders. Their eyes were so beautiful, she hated not being able to see them. But there was a reason, and after a moment, she remembered it. "It's to keep them from shying if they see something unexpected."

"You don't make Archie wear them! You don't even make him wear a bit."

Chess seemed to admire Joni for that, too. Maybe that was why the slave thing, the captive animal thing, didn't come up about Archie. "I can't *stop* him with a bit!" Joni could have said. She could have explained how strong the hackamore was. Carleen had said it was only okay to use because Joni was a kid. In the hands of an adult, it would be too harsh. But that was too much to get into.

"It's more dangerous if they shy when they're driving," she said. "And sometimes the cart scares them if they see it behind them."

"Then they shouldn't have to pull it!"

"They don't see it, so it doesn't scare them," Joni said. But Chess wasn't listening. The dogs were racing down from the farmyard to greet them. The border collies darted and circled. The Bears loomed and boomed, and waved their plumy tails.

"They're friendly," Joni said. But Chess seemed to know

what to do, which was to stand still and let the dogs come to her. She didn't bend and stare into their eyes. Instead, she held out her lightly closed fists for them to sniff, and only began patting them when all tails were wagging.

"Don't pat the Bears," Joni said. "They're disgusting."

"They're beautiful!" Chess rested her hand reverently on Tasha's rounded head. Joni could see the brown, ragged mop that was Tasha's belly, but maybe Chess couldn't. Tasha's eyes went melty and she stood still, soaking up the attention.

After several minutes, Joni pried Chess away from the dogs and took Archie to his stall. They both fed him carrots. Chess laughed, and when Archie rolled in the dirt, she laughed again. "Why does he do that?"

Archie stood up and shook. The dust flew in a cloud. "It scratches his itches," Joni said. "And dries up the sweat." Chess suddenly looked sober, but she didn't say anything, just followed Joni up to the hayloft.

The mother cat appeared, meowing. Joni climbed into the mow and headed toward the back wall. But the cat went off in a different direction, speaking sharply over her shoulder.

"She wants us to follow," Joni said. "She must have moved them again."

The kittens were now in a different hay bale cave, awake and crawling over one another. When Joni spoke, they turned their heads toward her. Joni picked up the gray-and-white one and handed him to Chess.

Chess's eyes widened. So did her mouth. She cradled the kitten gently, staring at him. "He's—Joni, he's *shaking*!"

"Purring. Listen."

Chess held the kitten closer to her face. She'd gone pale. "Oh, he's so—he's . . ." She went silent, taking the kitten in with all her being. Joni felt almost embarrassed. She scooped up the other three and bundled them into her lap. They were purring, too. They seemed to have learned overnight.

The cat gave one of the kittens a lick on the head. Then she raced to the edge of the mow and leaped down. Joni said, "Now we have to stay and babysit till she comes back." Not that there was any chance of Chess leaving. She looked completely enthralled.

Joni said, "She always has her kittens during haying, when the tractors are going in and out of here. So we end up bringing them indoors."

Chess looked up from the kitten she was holding. "You should spay her."

NINE

Fields

Joni's mouth fell open, but Chess didn't notice. She was completely absorbed in the kitten. She stroked it from head to tail with one finger, over and over. Her face was soft and joyful, but also sad.

"If we spayed her, we wouldn't have kittens," Joni said.

"That's the whole point!" Chess cupped the kitten against her belly, tenderly touching his pink toes. "Do you know how many unwanted cats there are?"

"We want ours," Joni said. "We always find them homes."

"Everybody says that—"

"But we *do* it!" Joni said. She felt completely free with Chess all of a sudden—free to disagree, free to interrupt. Because she and Chess were not that different. No matter what her opinions were, Chess was completely melted by this kitten.

She couldn't help it. She wasn't even trying.

"Danae has one of our last-year kittens," Joni said. "And Ray has one—you know, Ray, who touched the electric fence three times? You could have one, too, if you want."

Chess wanted the gray-and-white kitten. She wanted it more than anything. Joni knew the signs. But she shook her head. "We don't believe in owning animals. It's like owning slaves—"

"Oh, it *is* not!" Joni said. "We're *their* slaves! Do you know how early my dad gets up every day, just to feed the stupid sheep?"

"*And* take their milk! And make money from it!"

"Not a lot of money!" Joni said. "The cheese is famous and it's really expensive, but Dad has to run this whole farm to get it. He and the sheep are like partners."

"Except the sheep don't get to choose," Chess said.

Okay, Chess was right about that. But what kind of life would a sheep choose? "Sheep are demented," Joni said. "All they care about is food. If they were in charge, they'd eat grass all summer, and in winter they'd starve, without a farmer to feed them hay. And then there wouldn't be sheep anymore."

"Maybe that would be okay."

Joni had thought that more than once. Sheep ruled their lives on this farm. If the sheep got out, or got sick, or needed milking, or needed hay made for them, Dad was on it like a shot. Family had to fit in around the edges. But there was a big difference between her thinking that and Chess saying it.

She looked down at her lap. Her empty lap. While she'd focused on Chess, her three kittens had straggled across the bales in the direction their mother had gone. Their tiny, pointed tails stuck straight up. They'd only been alive for about four weeks, yet they were bravely striking off to see the world.

"Help!" Joni said. She and Chess blocked the wandering kittens with their arms and turned them toward each other. Like little windup toys, they just kept walking, lifting their tender paws high to avoid the prickly hay. One of the tigers bopped the gray-and-white kitten, and it tipped over in shock. So did the tiger.

Chess laughed, her deep, feeding-Archie-carrots chuckle. "They're so great! How can you not be out here all day long? *I* would—and I'd set up a kitten cam at night!"

She sprawled on her stomach, propping her chin on her hands. Joni joined her, and they watched the stumbling travels, slow fights, sudden nap attacks. Out in the yard, Dad talked to Mom. Then she drove off and Kevin, who made cheese on Fridays, drove in.

Finally, Joni heard a muffled, gargling meow. The cat appeared at the edge of the haymow, a large mouse dangling from her jaws. Swallows dive-bombed her as she trod across the bales, talking with her mouth full. She put the mouse down near the kittens and they bumbled around it, puzzled and excited. The cat stretched out on her side and blinked smugly at Joni and Chess.

"Why is she doing that?" Chess asked. "Why doesn't she eat it?"

"She wants them to see it," Joni said. "It's how they learn to hunt." That was a long way in the future, though. The kittens circled the mouse, poking it with their paws, sniffing it. Their eyes were wide and amazed. After a few minutes, the cat pulled herself up and went to the mouse. She picked it up, tossing it high in the air. Once, twice. Then she crouched over it and began to eat. Joni sat up and stuffed her fingers in her ears. She hated that crunching sound. Chess leaned closer, as fascinated as the kittens.

When she finished the mouse, the cat stretched out to give her kittens what they really wanted, milk. Chess leaned back on her elbows, staring up into the high rafters. Sunlight streamed in the cracks between the boards, sending shafts of light into the darkness. A swallow hovered, then settled on the rim of a nest. "This is amazing. Nobody lives like this!"

"*We* do," Joni said. "*I* do."

"No, people live in cities. Most people. You've got to admit, this is—historical. Like being in *Charlotte's Web* or something."

Where's Papa going with that ax? Joni thought. The famous first line of *that* book. "So how come you guys moved here?" she asked. "How come you bought a farm, if nobody lives this way?"

"It's my dad's fantasy," Chess said. "He's always wanted to live in an old house on a dirt road, where he can let Noah and me run loose like you do. My mom thinks it's crazy, but he's the one who gets to decide. She decided the last time they moved."

"I've never moved," Joni said. She couldn't imagine it. The farm was like family, like a third grandmother. "So what will you guys do with your fields?"

"Look at them!" Chess said. "They're beautiful!"

"But somebody has to hay them, or graze animals on them.

Otherwise, they won't be fields anymore. They'll grow up to brush."

"I guess my dad will just mow them with the lawnmower," Chess said.

"That'll take *forever*!" Joni said. "Besides, grass should feed something. It shouldn't just get mowed with a lawnmower! Fields like that should have animals—"

It came to her all in a second, like the apple falling on Newton's head, or a sheep spotting an open gate.

"*I* know!" she said. "You can start a horse rescue!"

TEN

Coal-Black Morgans

Chess's eyes widened. "A rescue?"

"Like Kalysta's!" Joni said. "You've got a barn and pastures. And they wouldn't be captive animals if you *rescued* them. Right?"

Chess's lips parted. She stared at Joni, and then past her, past the barn wall, as if she saw something huge and new and amazing. After a moment, she started to speak, then swallowed and pressed her lips together. Joni felt a shiver on the back of her neck. It was a genius idea, and she could tell that it had a powerful effect on Chess. But *what* effect? What was Chess seeing, out past the barn boards?

She turned to Joni at last, as if just waking up. "Who's Kalysta?"

"I told you," Joni said. "Didn't I? She has a horse rescue. Our 4-H volunteers there."

"So it's near here?" Chess asked.

"Yes. Kalysta's amazing. You could learn a lot—like, about feeding horses, and what can happen if you do it wrong. There's this horse, Hooper—" Joni's voice choked off. Hooper had foundered. His front feet were warped out of shape and he could barely walk, they hurt so much. If Chess could see Hooper, she'd understand how dangerous too much food could be for horses.

"We go on Sundays," she said. "You could come with us." Was Chess even listening? She was still staring through the wall. Joni waited. It would take time for Chess to think this through.

Dad appeared at the barn door. "There you are, kids! Listen—I'm taking the lambs to Mrs. Abernathy, and Kevin's so busy making cheese he wouldn't notice if you fell off the roof. Why don't you ride along with me? I can drop you off at home," he said, looking at Chess with raised eyebrows. Like Joni, he wasn't good at remembering names.

"Chess left her bike down in the field," Joni said, helping him out.

"Hop in the truck," Dad said. "We'll go get it."

In a wooden crate in the back of the pickup, two large lambs bleated and crowded each other, hunting for a way through the slats. Baby lambs were smart little daredevils, but at this age they started to turn stupid, and only wanted to do what every other sheep was doing.

Chess reached in to pat them. They shied away from her

hand. "They're going to live on our road?"

"For the summer," Dad said. "Then they'll live in Mrs. Abernathy's freezer!"

Dad, please! Joni thought.

Chess didn't say anything, just climbed into the cab beside Joni. They bounced across the field—not in silence, because Dad was talking, but Joni didn't listen and Chess just sat there, staring straight ahead. What was she thinking?

Dad put Chess's bike in the back with the lambs. Then he drove out to the main road, around a couple of corners, and turned onto North Valley Road. He didn't even slow down as they passed Chess's house. "Dad!" Joni said.

"No, this is a chance for Chess to meet another neighbor. Ruth is an interesting woman. You'll like her, Chess." Like he was doing everybody a favor! Joni slumped back against the seat. How awful was *this* going to be?

At Mrs. Abernathy's, Dad drove past the minis' shed and around to the back side of the house. A car and a pickup were parked there. Mrs. Abernathy sat on the deck, and an old man in coveralls was coming down the steps.

"I'll be back tomorrow to check on them," he said.

"No need!" Mrs. Abernathy said. The man didn't seem to hear. He nodded stiffly to Dad, and drove off in his truck.

Mrs. Abernathy met Dad's eyes and they started to laugh. "Do I *look* like a femme fatale?" Mrs. Abernathy said. "I ask you!" Then she sobered. "With three husbands pushing up daisies, I suppose that's just what I am! Old fools! They're all looking for somebody to take care of them. But I'm too old to get a puppy and I'm much too old to take on another man!"

She stood up, leaning on a cane. "I won't come out with you, if you don't mind. Tweaked this stupid hip yesterday, getting out of the cart."

Dad backed the pickup around to a small wooden pen with a lean-to roof, and a black rubber tub full of water. The field around it was divided into paddocks, fenced with electric netting. They radiated from the pen like slices of a pie.

"See, they'll have fresh grass every few days," Joni said. "As soon as they eat one pen down, they'll get another."

Chess nodded, her eyes wide and dark. Did she see that this was a good life for a sheep? Or did she only see that it was going to be a short one?

Dad backed the pickup into the pen, got out, and opened the crate. Each lamb made a spectacular leap off the tailgate and looked around with glazed, frantic eyes. Then one dropped its head and sampled the grass, almost by accident. The other shoved up against it, shoulder to shoulder, and started to eat, too.

"That was easy." Dad drove back to the house where Mrs. Abernathy waited, leaning on her cane.

"Is everything in order? I had to ask Reginald to set things up for me."

"Everything's fine. Are you all right?" Dad asked.

"*Phhh!*" Mrs. Abernathy flapped her hand, as if brushing away flies. "I'll be out in the garden again tomorrow! Do you have time to stop a minute? I have cookies. Bought, not made, but they're good."

"No, thanks!" Joni said quickly.

But Dad said, "I'd love a cookie!" and in a minute he was on the deck, raising the patio umbrella. Mrs. Abernathy sent Chess and Joni in for the tray. "You'll see it there on the table," she said. "There's a pitcher of milk in the refrigerator. Bring that, too, if you would."

It seemed dark inside the house, after the bright outdoors. Everything was neat and plain—an old person's house. Mrs. Abernathy had an old person's refrigerator, too, with hardly anything in it. Joni got the milk, turned, and gasped. From the back wall of the kitchen, a pair of black horses came splashing through shallow water, straight at her.

It was a photograph, poster-sized. The horses were harnessed to a four-wheeled metal carriage. The driver leaned forward from her seat, urging them on. On the back of the carriage, another woman leaned far out to the side. All four heads were at the exact same angle, all four faces fiercely focused on something just ahead of them. The driver was younger, plumper, with bright color in her cheeks, but . . .

"Chess, it's *her*! Those must be her Morgans!"

Chess was reading the cookie package. She put it back on the tray and looked at the photograph, but she didn't say anything.

Joni glanced around for pictures of the husbands. She spotted one photo near the phone, a young man in uniform. The picture was soft and dull, as if taken by a not-very-good camera a long time ago.

In the center of the table was a fresh, crisp photo of a man with a long jaw and no hair. He smiled as if someone had just cracked a joke, and the smile made Joni think she might like him. But she could tell he was sick when the picture was taken, and he looked faded, too. Not like the horses. She still wanted to dodge out of their way. That was a picture you could walk right into and live in. Maybe Mrs. Abernathy did sometimes, alone in this little house.

ELEVEN

Electric Fence

Joni picked up the tray and carried it out. Dad and Mrs. Abernathy sat at the table, talking. Dad's eyes sparkled the way they did when he was really interested in somebody. Joni would say he was flirting, except that Mrs. Abernathy was old.

Everybody drank, except Chess. Everybody nibbled crisp chocolate-orange cookies, except Chess. "Please!" Mrs. Abernathy said. "Pour yourself some milk!"

"I'm a vegan," Chess said.

"Vegan!" Mrs. Abernathy raised both eyebrows. "Vegetarian I understand. I was raised on a farm and I know what killing is. But why not milk, for instance? It doesn't hurt a cow to be milked!"

"What about her calf?" Chess asked. Her voice trembled

slightly, but it was sharp, too. Joni cringed inside. Answering back to Mrs. Abernathy? She could never do that!

Mrs. Abernathy said, "In my day, we taught the calves to drink from a pail, and we raised them."

"And then what?" Chess looked her straight in the face. Joni wouldn't have done that, either. Mrs. Abernathy seemed startled. She paused before she answered, choosing her words carefully.

"Some heifers came into our milk herd, and the rest were eaten, I suppose. I take your point. Milking doesn't harm a cow, but her calf is another matter. You want to avoid causing any degree of harm, and I can respect that. I'm only sorry I don't have anything vegan to offer you—other than white wine, and you're a little young for that! How about a glass of water?"

"You're going to eat those lambs, aren't you?" Chess said.

Joni's stomach lurched. She glanced at Dad, who was watching alertly.

Mrs. Abernathy's clear blue eyes seemed to flare with light. "Yes! I'm going to feed them all summer and fall, and then they're going to feed me. That's the bargain we've made with domesticated animals! We feed them, they feed us, and in the end, we all feed the grass that grows over our worn-out bodies. We accept that."

Chess was white-faced, but her chin was up. Her eyes met Mrs. Abernathy's. "*I* don't."

Mrs. Abernathy gave a bark of laughter. "Bless you, child, you know what you think, anyway! Why don't you two go look at the horses?"

They were being dismissed, like little kids! Chess hesitated for a second. Then she got up from the table. Joni followed, feeling that she'd just had a narrow escape.

The minis were dozing indoors, away from the warm sun and the flies. They wore their grazing muzzles, baskets made of nylon straps that hung over their mouths. Joni missed being able to see their adorable noses, but grazing muzzles were a great idea. They reduced the amount of grass a horse could eat. A little bit stuck through the basketwork, so horses could nibble all day without getting fat. Maybe she should get one for Archie.

The barn was only a garden shed, but it was the perfect size for minis. Half held hay and equipment. The other half was set up as a run-in, with a gate so they could be closed inside. There were two tie rings, very close to the ground, and two salt bricks in wall-mounted holders, one white and one the red, mineral kind. You were supposed to give horses a choice of salt, but Joni didn't know anyone who did. Mrs. Abernathy did everything by the book—

"Poor babies," Chess whispered. "Look how depressed they are!"

"*What?*" The minis stood with their heads low and their eyes were half-shut. "They're *asleep!*" Joni said.

Kubota lifted his head and pricked his ears at her. After a moment, he walked over and put his nose up. His long whiskers, sticking out between the crisscrossed straps of the muzzle, trembled pitifully. Joni laughed. "You are *so* not starving!"

"Those things are *horrible!*" Chess said. "They should be running free, like the mustangs! They should be eating that grass—" She pointed to the lush grass growing outside the door.

"They'd eat themselves to *death!*" Joni said. "You don't

understand. Horses *can't* have too much grass. They'll founder—"

But how could she explain founder? It was one of the strange things about horses, that eating too much could hurt their feet. Fatally hurt their feet. She'd need a diagram to show how the inner lining of the hoof swelled up, with no place to go because it was contained inside the hard hoof wall. She would have to explain how a foundered horse shuddered and sweated in pain, how he tried not to put any weight on his front feet. And how could she do that when Chess wouldn't listen? Instead she was pulling fistfuls of grass.

Kubota followed her along the inside of the electric fence. JD joined him, nickering as Chess straightened with a large armful. "See how hungry they are!"

"They're horses. Of course they're hungry! Watch out!" Chess was reaching over the fence to give Kubota the grass. "That's electric," Joni said.

Chess stepped back. "It looks like string."

"It is string, but it's got electric wire running through it. Here, give me the grass. I'll put it inside for them." Normally, Joni wouldn't open somebody else's gate, or feed their animals without asking, but nothing was normal about this visit. She took hold of the plastic gate hooks. The wire sagged, and Kubota stepped toward the gate. Quickly, Joni tossed the grass in and closed it. Animals! They looked like they were paying no attention, but open a gate, only for a second, and even a sheep was smart enough to take advantage.

Chess put her hand on the top gate hook. "I don't feel anything."

"You would if you touched the wire!"

"Really? How bad is it?" Chess put her finger on the black-and-white twine. There was a loud snapping sound. A spark flew, the minis bolted, and Chess fell down, all in the same instant.

Joni dropped to her knees beside her. "Are you okay? Chess?"

Chess sat up, rubbing her elbow. "Ow," she said after a moment. "Okay—*ow!*" Tears started to trickle down her cheeks.

"I'm sorry," Joni said. It wasn't her fault, but she felt like it was. Getting zapped by a fence was horrible. It hurt you all over, and worst at the nearest large joint, which made no sense to Joni even after Dad explained it to her. Should she give Chess a hug? But maybe Chess didn't like hugs. Not everyone did. "You're not going to do it again, right? I mean, you're smarter than Ray, right?"

Chess raised her eyes to look at the minis. They huddled in the middle of the paddock, pricking their ears warily.

"How often does it happen to *them*?"

"Never. I mean—hardly ever. Animals learn fast. All they have to do is touch the fence once."

"Really?"

"Yes!" Joni said. "Even sheep! They practically never touch it. You're okay, right?"

Chess stood up, hugging her arm close to her body. She nodded, but Joni knew how she really felt. The deep ache would last for hours. So would the hurt feelings—which was silly. A fence wasn't a person. It didn't shock you on purpose. But it felt like someone you trusted had suddenly knocked you down. Did animals feel that way? They acted as if they did. The sheep always had—well, you had to call it *shocked*—looks on their faces as they raced away.

"It keeps them in," she said, answering what Chess must be thinking. "It keeps them safe."

"But—*baby lambs*? You let *baby lambs* touch that?"

Joni nodded. She didn't think most lambs ever did touch the fence, actually. They must learn from their mothers that a fence was something to stay away from, without knowing why. But some must touch it, and it must be awful for them. "It's better than being eaten," she said.

Chess turned dark eyes on her. "They're going to get eaten, anyway."

"Yes, but . . . coyotes . . ." Chess had never seen a lamb that had been torn apart by coyotes. She didn't understand.

Dad drove up just then. They got into the truck, and he dropped Chess off at her house. "Wow," he said after a moment. "That's one opinionated kid."

Joni didn't know whether to defend Chess or agree. Or maybe just nod. Nodding worked. Dad took the hint and didn't ask questions. They drove home, where they found an old white van with New York license plates in the yard, and Olivia getting out.

TWELVE

A Dog Crate

Olivia's face lit up when she saw them. She ran over and hugged Joni, then Dad, and turned back toward the van as two other people got out, a short dark-haired girl Olivia's age, and a tall young man. Joni did remember Rosita, sort of, from the crowd of friends at Olivia's graduation. But who was this guy?

Olivia said, "Daddy, Joni, you remember Rosita, right? And this is Tobin, a friend of hers from high school. We visited him last night, and it turns out he's studying soil carbon and looking for a farm internship this summer. So he decided to bring us the rest of the way and talk to you. Isn't that amazing!"

Joni didn't think it was all that amazing. Olivia was beautiful, tall and slim with honey-colored hair like Dad and long, tanned legs. The guy, Tobin, wasn't staring at her, but Joni could see that he had to work at it. He'd grown up on a small farm, he told Dad, and gotten interested in soil science, but now he wanted some practical experience to give him some perspective.

"Well, you just delivered my two substitute interns," Dad said, "but it's haying season, so it's easy to tempt me. Come in and have lunch, and let's talk about it."

They talked about it. And talked. Afterward, Olivia showed Tobin and Rosita around the farm, and they all talked some more. It would be a long time before Joni had Olivia to herself, she could see.

Tobin stayed for supper, too—hummus, chips, and wine, brought by Rosita, grilled lamb and a green salad from Mom's garden, with last year's cheese crumbled on top, and lots more talk—Dad and Olivia, mostly, explaining more about the farm. "Amazing!" Rosita kept saying. Tobin just took it in, eyes wide and shining. But every time Olivia stopped talking, he asked her a question, a smart question, about pasture rotation or cheese. The questions made Olivia look at him, and pretty soon the whole supper seemed to be about the two of them getting to know each other. Joni sat picking off flecks of cheese rind and feeding them to the dogs, until suddenly she felt an arm around her shoulders.

She looked up, and Mom smiled down at her with a look that said, "I know!"

"So, Jon-Jon!" Olivia said, interrupting herself. "What's been going on for you?"

Sixth-grade graduation? Chess yelling at Mrs. Abernathy? "Kittens," Joni said.

Olivia's face lit up. "In the barn? Show me in the morning, okay?"

"Okay." Maybe Tobin would be gone by then.

But by breakfast, it had been decided that Tobin wasn't leaving. Olivia and Rosita had the barn apartment, where the interns usually stayed, but Dad said he could park his van, which was also a camper, in the yard. Joni saw Mom roll her eyes. She liked privacy. Dad was a more-the-merrier kind of person, especially in haying season.

Fewer people would be fine with Joni right now. Like, subtract Rosita and Tobin! Without them, Olivia wouldn't be talking about how grazing animals could put carbon back in the soil and even reverse climate change, about grass-fed this and pastured that. "It's just the way I was brought up," she said. "I never realized we were activists until I went to college."

Joni mopped up the last of her egg with a bit of English muffin. It was the way she was brought up, too. This egg came from a hen that got to run around outdoors and scratch in the dirt. But it was just an egg. It was just the way they lived. How was it being an activist? It didn't comfort the afflicted, or afflict the comfortable.

"Olivia, let's go see the kittens," she said.

"I've seen them!" Olivia said. "Their mom moved them into the apartment at two o'clock this morning! Rosita's not a cat person, so guess whose bed they're on!"

"It's time they came in the house, anyway," Dad said. "I'm going to cut hay this morning."

"Come on, Jon-Jon, I'll help you bring them over."

Finally! Some time for just the two of them. Joni followed Olivia out to the apartment. It was one rustic room, with a sink, a stove, a table and chairs, and bunk beds. The kittens were exploring the unmade bottom bunk, their tails upright with excitement.

Olivia made her hand into a spidery monster, creeping over the blankets. The gray-and-white kitten arched his back, fluffing his tail and the hair along his spine. He spat at the scary hand, then hauled off and smacked it with his tiny paw.

"Oh, honey, you're really scared, aren't you?" Olivia picked him up, stroking and soothing him.

"Doesn't he have a great purr?" Joni said. "I have a new friend who really likes him, but . . . she can't have pets."

"Allergies?"

"No, they don't . . . they don't believe in keeping captive animals. They're vegans."

Olivia's eyebrows rose. "Really? Most people who use that term are talking about zoo animals. I mean, my vegan friends all have cats! But I guess if you're a purist . . ."

A purist. That was Chess. Joni said, "She's an activist, too."

"And she's your age? Because a sixth-grade activist—"

"We're not sixth graders anymore," Joni said.

"That's right! Congratulations! But who is this kid? Where is she from?"

"California. They moved into the white house on North Valley Road, and—she's really into animal rescue."

Olivia frowned. "Animal rescue, or animal rights?"

"Um—I don't know. Why?"

"Rescuers help animals who are in trouble. Some of the

rights people think they're *all* in trouble, that they should have never been domesticated. They get people's farm animals taken away, for, like, being kept outdoors! And they let lab animals out of cages."

"But—" Joni said. "I mean, poor mice!"

"I know," Olivia said. "I have mixed feelings about that one. Still—what's your friend's name?" She pulled out her phone.

"Chess—I mean, Francesca. Ventura. I think." Joni's stomach felt cold. She watched Olivia's thumbs hover, tap, hover.

"Yeah, Ventura," Olivia said. *Tap tap tap.* A tiger kitten was drawn to the sound. It crept toward the phone, ears flattened, chin high, ready to kill.

Olivia made the scary hand shape. The kitten shot a foot into the air, hissing. Joni gathered it in. It felt like it was made of wires. She kissed and cuddled it, coaxing out a purr. Chess loved these kittens, but she also thought they shouldn't exist. Maybe no animals should exist, except in the wild—but that wasn't working out so well for wild animals, and—

"Oh, boy!" Olivia said. "You'd better see this." She turned the phone around.

A headline read, "ANIMAL RIGHTS GROUP PROTESTS CIRCUS." The picture underneath was confusing—a lot of people standing around a large plastic dog crate. Joni could see a lime-green shape inside it. Beside the crate, a sleek-haired older woman wearing a ringmaster's red coat faced the camera. The hair and the dark eyes seemed familiar, very familiar.

The text read:

Selina Bowman, prominent animal rights activist, exhibited her twelve-year-old granddaughter in a dog crate outside the Page Brothers Circus yesterday to protest the mistreatment of animals. "(She) volunteered to do this," Ms. Bowman said. "I'm very proud of her."

But the child's father, Paul Ventura, who received word of his daughter's involvement in the protest from multiple friends via social media, arrived twenty minutes after the protest began and removed her. He declined to comment for this story.

Below the text was a second photo. A girl in a lime-green T-shirt, artfully layered over another shirt, walked beside a tall man. Her face had been digitally blurred, but Joni knew those thin shoulders. She knew that hairstyle. "When did this happen?"

Olivia reached for the phone. "Back in February."

Just a few months ago. Was this why Chess's family had moved all the way across the country?

"If she pulls some kind of stunt like that on this farm, it could be damaging," Olivia said. "Daddy doesn't need any weird publicity. Does she come here a lot, your friend?"

"She came once," Joni said. "To see the kittens." Her voice sounded funny. She cleared her throat. "She *loved* them."

"Well—hey, Joni!" Olivia gave her a quick hug. "It's probably okay. She's just a kid. Maybe she was being manipulated."

No, Joni thought. If Chess got into that crate, it was because she thought it was the right thing to do. It was exactly like her.

They carried the kittens to the house, with the mother cat twining around their ankles, meowing anxiously. Joni put them in her room and watched them explore their new planet, full of alien things like shoes, hairbrushes, and horse models. The kittens sniffed and challenged each new item. Their tiny earnest tails stuck straight in the air, fluffed out like miniature bottlebrushes.

The mother lay watching, but as soon as Joni opened the door, she snatched up a kitten by the scruff of its neck and darted through. Joni caught her and stuffed her back inside. "Sorry. They have to be captive animals for a while."

She was met with an accusing, green-eyed stare.

"I get it, I get it!" Joni said. "But it beats them getting squished, okay? Anyway, you should be spayed. You know that, right?"

The cat stared for a moment more, then turned away as if Joni was a moron and scratched at the door again.

THIRTEEN

Patrick

Joni spent a lot of the day on kittens. Messages from Chess piled up, and Chess would love watching for that earnest, I-need-to-poop-right-now expression, and swooping kittens into litter boxes. But Joni didn't call her back.

The dog crate was what Chess meant by being an activist, not eating a free-range egg. Joni wasn't supposed to know about the dog crate. How was she going to deal with that? Putting it off until tomorrow was the best she could come up with.

That night, the kittens kept her awake for a long time, exploring, getting lost, squeaking to each other, then finding her and purring like electric razors. It was the most exciting night of their lives, and a long one for Joni. When she woke up, everyone else had eaten breakfast, and before she could finish hers, it was time to go to Kalysta's. She had meant to ask Chess to come, to see what a horse rescue was like. But now she wasn't sure, and anyway, it was too late.

The three teenagers—Li Min, Willow, and Tod—were already at Kalysta's when Joni and Danae arrived, looking at the horses in the paddocks. "Anybody new?" Danae asked.

No, but there was one horse Joni didn't see. Her stomach knotted. "Where's Hooper?"

"He was getting better," Danae said quickly. "I'm sure—no, look, she's bringing him out."

Kalysta was large and hardly ever moved quickly, but even she had to slow down for Hooper. The big pinto leaned back as he walked, keeping his weight off his front feet. His hind feet stepped far under his body, trying to bear all the weight. Walking was still torture for Hooper. Standing was torture, too, so he lay down a lot, and his tail was full of shavings. Kalysta led him to the closest paddock, next to the barn. When his halter was off, Hooper shook himself and hobbled to his hay net.

"That looks a little better," Willow said. "Last week, he would have just stood there."

Kalysta let herself back through the gate. "The vet's coming tomorrow, so we'll see. If he doesn't make real improvement soon, I'll have to make a decision."

Joni knew what kind of decision. It wasn't fair to keep Hooper alive if he had to be in terrible pain.

"Don't give up the ship, kiddo," Kalysta said. "There's a new treatment the vets at Countryside want to try. They're somewhat hopeful."

"Countryside's expensive," Tod said—a long speech from

him. He dug into his jeans pocket—they all did—and change chuckled into the donation jar, a horse supplement bottle stapled to the side of the barn.

"Thank you, Colts and Fillies!" Kalysta said. "You're the best. Hey, before you get to work, I have an announcement."

They all turned. The sun blazed off Kalysta's hair. This week, it was parrot red, with parrot-blue and parrot-green streaks. "Good thing horses are color-blind," Li Min murmured.

"It's positive news for a change," Kalysta said. "Any guesses? Starts with a *p*?"

Joni's mouth dropped open. She looked at Danae.

"*Patrick?*" Li Min shrieked. "You *got* him?" Kalysta nodded, and everybody started jumping and slapping high fives. Even Tod let out a hoot.

"Where is he?" Li Min said. "I want to meet him! We've been hearing about him for so long!"

"Out back," Kalysta said. "Wait! Walk quietly with me, okay? He's only been here for a couple of days, and he hasn't met a big group yet."

Joni tried to slow herself down, but she was ahead as they went around the corner. *"Oh!"* She stopped short. The others crowded against her, and she heard several gasps.

In the shady back paddock, a dark horse stood eating hay. His coat was dull, and all his bones showed. *All* his bones. Joni could see the knobs of his spine, and every rib, and the deep, deep hollows over his eyes. It felt almost embarrassing, like she was seeing something she wasn't supposed to see. They'd known his story for what seemed like months now. His elderly owner had sold him before she died. After a few months, the new owner's neighbors stopped seeing Patrick in the pasture and assumed he'd been sold. Then one of them went into the barn to borrow a tool and found him in a manure-packed stall. He hadn't been outside for more than a year.

"I thought the sheriff was feeding him!" Tod said.

"She was," Kalysta said. "This represents improvement, believe it or not!"

Patrick tore hay from the net with steady concentration. Eating mattered. It mattered terribly. But he turned his head to look at them as he chewed. He snatched another bite, then left the net to walk toward them.

"Oh, *sweetheart*! Can you believe it?" Kalysta said. "As hungry as he is? But he wants to see who you are, even more than he wants to eat."

Joni leaned on the top rail. Patrick sniffed her hands and then her face, gently and politely. His eyes were soft and curious. Joni held still, feeling his trembling whiskers on her cheek. After a moment, he glanced toward his hay net. He wanted to go back to it, but he chose to stay with her.

"He's wonderful," Joni said. "He's a grown-up!"

"Yes," Kalysta said. "He has beautiful manners. All right, kids, off to work. Let's not keep this sweet boy from his lunch."

Joni grabbed a fork and wheelbarrow and started cleaning Hooper's stall. "Can we go kill that woman?" she heard Willow say from the next stall. "Like, *now*? I was half-asleep till I saw him. Now I'm like, Adrenaline Girl! With a pitchfork!"

"I want to lock her up somewhere," Tod said.

"In the dark," said Li Min. "Next door to a pizza joint."

Joni didn't talk, just worked her way steadily from stall to stall. A deep fluffy bed for Hooper. A fragrant flake of hay for Patrick. A fresh salt block in the donkey's stall, sparkling clear water in all the buckets. She wanted every corner of every stall to say, *Life is sweet. People care for you. We'll make amends.*

But was she just trying to make up for a basic deal that was bad for horses, all horses? A line from one of Dad's favorite songs played over and over in Joni's head: *And before I'll be a slave I'll be buried in my grave, and go home to my Lord and be free.* Maybe instead of cleaning stalls and filling water buckets, she should be turning the horses loose.

But what about the cars whizzing by on the road? What about the cornfield next door? Hooper would finish eating himself to death there. He didn't understand why his feet hurt. The rest would join him or be killed on the highway. The world where horses could run loose and take care of themselves didn't exist anymore, at least not around here. That world had sparse grasses that the horses gnawed down as soon as it appeared. Always moving, always munching, they stayed lean and healthy.

But didn't slave owners say things like that? *They wouldn't know how to take care of themselves. They need us—*

Shut up, she told the voice in her head. It sounded a lot like Chess.

Kalysta's phone rang, and she answered. "A hay donation? Yes, Becky, absolutely! Seventy-five bales—wonderful! Let me see if I can find someone to store it for me." There was no room for extra hay in this barn. Even the office had been turned into a stall. Kalysta took the phone into her new office, a camper-trailer parked outside. "Come out when you're done," she told the 4-Hers.

Half an hour later, they all crowded into the camper. Still on the phone, Kalysta raised a finger. "One minute," she meant, but Joni knew better than to believe that. She pried off her boots and climbed onto a bunk.

Danae flopped beside her. "The fundraising thermometer's gone *down*."

"It costs a lot to take care of Hooper." Joni was looking at the EVERY HORSE NEEDS A JOB poster. It had pictures cut out of magazines, showing horses at work. There was a police horse, a city carriage horse, even a pony doing Agility, jumping through a hoop just like a dog, with his owner directing him from the ground. "Bottom line," Kalysta had said, "if they know how to do something people find useful, they're less likely to end up here."

Slaves were useful, too . . .

Shut up! Anyway, Chess was wrong. If owning horses was slavery, Kalysta wouldn't be for it. She loved horses more than anything. She didn't have a husband or family. She did bookkeeping to get by, and she did this. That was why she'd made the HOW TO NOT BE A CRAZY HORSE-LADY poster, in her favorite orange marker. The rules included:

- *Don't fill every available space with horses.*
- *In case of an emergency, put on your own oxygen mask before helping others. This means YOU, Kalysta! Fully fund your retirement account!!!*

- *Know that you are not the only person who can love and care for your horses.*
- *Don't confuse love with care. Horses can't eat love, and it doesn't clean the stalls.*

"Hang up, Kalysta," Willow murmured under her breath. But you couldn't hurry somebody who wanted to give you seventy-five bales of hay. Joni looked for a Becky on the ANGELS poster, Kalysta's list of people who had helped. Their group was there, Colts and Fillies 4-H Club. Dad was there, and—

Wow, so was Ruth Abernathy! Her name was written in glitter pen, an honor reserved for Super-Angels who gave a large amount of money or time. There was a sliding scale. The homeless lady who donated five dollars of her bottle deposit money once a month was also written up in glitter. Mrs. Abernathy's name was in the middle of the list, so she'd been an Angel for a while.

"Phew!" Kalysta hung up the phone, rose from the table, and scribbled "Hay Bank" on the bottom of the WISH LIST poster in magenta.

"What's a hay bank?" Danae asked.

"It's like a food bank," Kalysta said. "A food bank provides free food for people who are short of money. A hay bank does the same thing for people who run into problems and can't feed their animals. I'd start one if I had the money, or the time, or the space."

"Where does the hay come from?" Joni asked.

"People donate it, or give money to buy it. Having a place to store the hay is just as important, though. People who have animals usually need the space for their own hay."

"Maybe *we* could start a hay bank," Li Min said. "As a group project?"

Joni opened her mouth and closed it. She knew of a barn with no animals in it. She knew some huge fields with no one to hay them. But she had no idea if Chess would go for it.

"I would love it if you guys would take that on," Kalysta said. "But it's a major amount of work. Look before you leap—"

"Like you always do!" Willow said.

"Exactly! Meanwhile, here's the scoop on Patrick."

When he'd been found, the case had gone before a judge, who ordered his owner to feed him properly. The sheriff came a few times a week to make sure that happened, and Patrick was left where he was while the state and the owner's lawyer did some legal maneuvering.

"But Ruth Abernathy knew the first owner," Kalysta said. "She was pretty sure Patrick had only been leased to this new woman. That would make him the property of the first owner's heirs. She tracked them down, and they found a copy of the lease agreement and authorized me to take the horse. And you know what? The woman who starved him *cried* when he left!"

"*I'd* like to make her cry!" Willow said.

Kalysta shook her head. "I have to believe mental illness is involved there. It's not uncommon. I hope this woman gets help. But I have to do my part, which is to take care of the horses who get caught in the middle."

"I wish we could just take animals away from people like that!" Danae said.

"That cuts both ways!" Kalysta said. "Who gets to decide if an animal is being abused? Okay, with Patrick, it's obvious. But there are people who think riding is abuse. Should they have the right to take your horse away from you? *I* don't think so, but I guarantee there are people sitting in meetings right now, working on making that happen!"

People like Chess. Joni was glad she'd decided not to bring her—but was that smart? Kalysta was exactly the right person to talk to Chess. She didn't let people interrupt her, but she didn't get mad, either, and she could always think of the right words. *Who gets to decide . . .* That was good. Joni could try to say that, too, but even better, she had to get Chess over here the Sunday after camp. Then maybe she wouldn't have to spend the whole summer hearing about Mrs. Abernathy's horses!

FOURTEEN

A Lesson

Chess had called while Joni was away, wanting to come see the kittens again. But when Joni called back, no one answered. No one answered later in the day, either, and after supper, Joni decided she'd better ride. Camp started in less than a week, and what had she done to get ready? Pretty much exactly nothing.

When she was serious about riding, she worked in the flat place below the barn. She thought of it as her ring, but it had no fence, and Archie had no interest in trotting around in circles. He kept veering off in more creative directions. When Joni corrected him for the fourth time, he gave a tiny buck. Joni grabbed for the saddle horn. "You *brat!*"

Someone laughed. Joni turned to see Mrs. Abernathy standing there and leaning on her cane with both hands—not like she needed it to stand up, but like she planned to stay where she was for some time.

"Pardon me, but would you like a riding lesson?" she asked. Joni hesitated, and Mrs. Abernathy said, "You need one!"

Joni felt herself go red. She didn't need anybody to point that out. "I have 4-H camp next week."

"Good! There are three things I can teach you, any one of which will move you up a level. Are you game?"

Joni wasn't game. She was a wimp—too much of a wimp to admit that she wasn't game. She nodded.

"Good for you!" Mrs. Abernathy said. "Come over here, and I'll show you what I mean."

Why is she even here? Joni wondered. Did she drive the minis? But, no, Mrs. Abernathy's car was parked near the milk house.

Archie went over to her gladly. A new person usually meant admiration, treats, and time to rest. Mrs. Abernathy let him sniff her hands and face, but she was looking over Joni's tack. Not clean. At camp, Joni would soap it every day, hoping to pass Stable Inspection. But this was home, not camp.

"Has anyone ever talked with you about using your weight as an aid?" Mrs. Abernathy asked.

The aids were how you told a horse what you wanted him to do. Joni could ace a Quiz Bowl question on them. *What are the natural aids?* Hands, legs, seat. *What are the artificial aids?* Whip, spurs . . . Weight had something to do with the seat, but Joni didn't get it. You weighed what you weighed, right? You couldn't change that just to influence a horse.

"No," she said.

"They never do," Mrs. Abernathy said. "Listen—good riding happens in your core, in your spinal column. Not in your arms and legs. When you sit right, all you'll have to do is think of turning and your horse will do it. At least it will feel that way, and it will seem that way to anyone watching. If you can do that—and I'll bet you can—it should impress the heck out of them at 4-H camp!"

Joni had impressed people the wrong way last year. "What do I have to do?"

That was the beginning of a long evening. The blue of the sky deepened and darkened. One by one, Mom and Dad, Olivia, Tobin, and Rosita came to sit on the grassy bank and watch while Joni sank into Archie's back and became part of him.

That was what it felt like by the time Mrs. Abernathy let her ride. First, there was a lot of sitting still, refining her position in the saddle.

"Sit on your hands," Mrs. Abernathy said. "Now rock forward and back. Do you feel two bones poking down through your buns? Those are your seat bones. Think of them as flashlights, and point them straight down at the ground."

Next, she showed Joni how to bring her leg back so she was almost standing in the saddle, not sitting like in a chair. "Now sit up straight—no, don't arch your back. What are your flashlights doing?"

They were pointing backward. "Experiment," Mrs. Abernathy said. "How straight can you sit and still keep your flashlights pointing down? No," she told Archie, pulling her sleeve out of his mouth. "You're not allowed to do that. That's better, Joni. Now let's think about your center of gravity."

There was much, much more. Joni felt like a hunk of clay being shaped by Mrs. Abernathy. *Lengthen this, push that, breathe deeply, bring your leg back again.* At first, she couldn't forget that everybody was watching, but soon she was working too hard to remember. Bit by bit, Mrs. Abernathy took her apart and hooked her back together again so she felt strong and solid. All without Archie taking a step! How was this a riding lesson?

Finally, Mrs. Abernathy said, "Walk him in a circle, and notice how that feels."

It felt like Archie was one of these flotation-device horses little kids wear around their middles. Instead of just sitting on top of him, Joni seemed to be way down inside him. She felt springy and alive in the saddle, and Archie's walk rippled from the soles of her feet all the way to her head.

"Don't look down!" Mrs. Abernathy called. "Head high, remember your flashlights, and look to your left."

Joni glanced left. Mrs. Abernathy said, "No, not like that! Imagine that you have eyes in your upper chest, and look with *them*. Turn your head and your upper body, and look straight at the place you want to go."

Eyes in her chest. Joni turned them, and Archie turned at the same time.

"Now turn right! Aim, *intend*, and go."

The two sets of eyes organized Joni's whole body. It felt like martial arts, not riding. Archie immediately turned right, like they shared the same body. "Wow!"

"Exactly!" Mrs. Abernathy said. "Look where you want to go, with intention, and the horse will go there. Circle him around me—that's right! Now commit to that arc. Keep looking a quarter of the way ahead of you, all the way around your circle."

Joni obeyed. It was the same circle, but she felt completely different—taller, straighter, in command. She *felt* the way Mrs. Abernathy looked. Her hands and legs hardly had to do anything. It really was like she and Archie were one—

No, they weren't! At the barn side of the circle, Archie barged straight ahead, ignoring Joni's head turn and her seat. Mrs. Abernathy laughed. "Typical pony! Always ready to take you down a peg! Put more weight on that inside seat bone, and *look*, and turn, and look—"

Joni put everything she had into her seat bone, her head turn, her solid, fluid seat. With a snort, Archie settled back on track.

"Beautiful!" Mrs. Abernathy called. "Stop and give him a big pat."

Joni collapsed on Archie's neck, hugging him. "I didn't use the reins at all—did I? I can't remember."

"You didn't use the reins!" Mrs. Abernathy was smiling, and Joni could see why all those old men wanted to marry her.

But, wow—camp was going to be different this year! Was that completely good? Archie had humiliated her last year, but he'd also made her special. "You're that little kid with the gray pony?" people kept saying. "I wish I were that brave!"

"I don't want him to get too good," she said.

Mrs. Abernathy let out a crack of laughter. "No worries, my friend, you still have a lot to learn! But you absorbed something important tonight. You'll lose that feeling, of course, but now that you know what it is, you'll be able to figure out how to get it back, and you'll start having a lot more fun. This is a fine pony. You could do anything on him!"

"He's *amazing*!" Joni said. Her chest swelled with love and pride.

Dad came up. He squeezed Joni's knee and gave Archie a scratch on the chest. "Bravo, you guys!"

Mrs. Abernathy said, "Sorry, I didn't mean to take over your evening."

"No, that was interesting to watch," Dad said. "Even for me, and I'm not a horse person."

"Agreed," Mom said, kissing Archie's nose. "But put him away, Joni. Ruth brought us a strawberry-rhubarb pie, and you ladies have certainly earned your slices!"

Mrs. Abernathy turned toward the picnic table, then paused to look back at Joni. "I know you'll clean that tack before camp," she said. "But I was a stable inspector back in the day, and I'll let you in on a secret. Buckle gunk! That's all I'm willing to say, but I think you'll figure out what it means."

"Buckle gunk," Joni repeated. She would check that out tomorrow.

Fifteen minutes later, she was at the picnic table next to Mrs. Abernathy, smelling like Archie and happily eating pie. "It might be on the sour side," Mrs. Abernathy warned. "Rhubarb is free. Strawberries cost money."

Joni made a happy noise with her mouth full. The pie was perfectly balanced between sour and sweet. Even the crust tasted good, and crust was not usually Joni's favorite part of a pie. "Thank you," she said, spraying crumbs.

"I brought it to thank your father for delivering my lambs,"

Mrs. Abernathy said. "But mostly it was an excuse to come here. I miss farming more than almost anything."

"What part of farming?" Tobin asked.

"Working that hard," Mrs. Abernathy said. "Haying—three thousand bales in the barn and I'd handled half of them, and I could still walk upright! And I miss the livestock."

"*Sheep?*" Joni asked. Could anyone miss sheep?

"We had cattle," Mrs. Abernathy said, "but the bargain is the same. Your relationship is with the whole herd. You keep them, they keep you. You make their lives sweet, and that sweetness flows into their milk . . ." She made a face. "Sorry, that's too poetic. I know what it's like to be up to here in manure, fixing an electric fence for the third time in an afternoon! Still—I'd trade almost everything I've experienced to be back in my twenties and farming."

Three husbands, Joni thought. *A pair of coal-black Morgans.*

"We have kittens," she said, doing her new, change-the-subject thing.

"Ah!" Mrs. Abernathy put her head on one side. "Spoken for? My late husband didn't care for cats. I'm ready to have one again."

"None of them have homes yet that I'm aware of," Mom said.

Mrs. Abernathy said, "Pick me out the slow one, Joni. The one that's shy and not as bright as the rest. It's going to be an indoor cat, so I don't want it to figure out what it's missing."

"But your house is way back from the road," Joni said.

"In my experience, the moment you fall in love with a cat it starts hurling itself under cars, no matter how far you live from the road! But my main reason is that I have a healthy population of songbirds, and I want to keep them."

"Okay," Joni said. So, not Chess's kitten . . .

As if she heard Joni's thought, Mrs. Abernathy asked, "Is your friend taking one?"

"They don't believe in captive animals," Joni heard herself say. Immediately, she wished she hadn't. Mrs. Abernathy's eyebrows lifted, and then *she* changed the subject.

FIFTEEN

Sheep

The next day during breakfast, the phone rang. Joni answered, and Chess said, "Can I come see them again?" She sounded breathless.

"Um—sure," Joni said, looking at Olivia. She wasn't paying attention. "When?"

"Well—I'm almost there."

Joni looked out the window. Down on the field, a small figure in a lime-green shirt leaned over the handlebars of a bike, toiling along the ruts. Her leg strokes were wobbly but getting more powerful. "Okay, I'll meet you." Joni swallowed the last of her toast and headed for the door. "Chess is coming," she said over her shoulder.

That got Olivia's attention. She glanced at Dad, who

shrugged. Olivia must have showed him the dog crate picture, but he didn't seem too worried.

Joni walked down to the level spot near the barn. The gravel was marked with Archie's tracks. Remembering the lesson, she turned, looking with the eyes in her chest, and twirled back around as Chess stopped the bike beside her. "Mrs. Abernathy gave me a riding lesson last night."

"Mrs. Abernathy?"

"The miniature horse lady." Joni took a deep breath. She had to try again. Mrs. Abernathy deserved it. "Look, she knows a *lot* about horses. I'm sure she's taking really good care—"

But Chess was on her way to the barn.

"They're not there anymore," Joni said. "We moved them into the house. But Mrs. Abernathy—"

Chess veered toward the house. *Never mind! Just never mind,* Joni thought. Chess was never going to listen to her. It was a job for Kalysta. "My room is this way," she said.

Her room wasn't the cleanest ever, and it wasn't cool, like Alyssa's. No ballet posters, no TV, no bright paint. The walls still had the same bunny wallpaper as when it was Olivia's room.

But Chess looked only at the kittens on their bookcase jungle gym. Joni forgot everything else, too, laughing until her sides ached. When the kittens seemed inclined to nap, she found a piece of baling twine—it was that kind of bedroom—and dragged it for them. That was too frightening, like some kind of hairy anaconda. Even the gray-and-white kitten hissed.

"What is it?" Chess asked.

"You mean the *baling twine*?" How could Chess not know

what baling twine was? It was the most common thing on a farm. If you couldn't fix something with baling twine or duct tape, you were really in trouble!

A kitten started scratching in the litter box. "Uh-oh," Joni said. "It's going to get stinky in here. C'mon, I'll show you."

Out at the barn, she explained how the baler compacted the hay and tied it tightly together with two lengths of twine.

"Do you use it over again?" Chess asked.

"No." Joni pointed to the mountain of used twine on the barn floor. "Dad burns it on the brush pile."

"Could I have some, then?"

"Sure," Joni said. "What for?"

"A project. I might need a lot—like that whole pile."

Obviously, she didn't want to say what the project was. Joni felt uncomfortable again. She hadn't made a new friend in a while, but she didn't remember it being like this—perfectly easy one minute, and the next minute . . . not.

Downstairs, a sheep baaed. "What's that?" Chess asked.

"One of the ewes hurt her leg. Dad's keeping her in for a while."

"What's a—"

"Ewe. It sounds like *you*—y-o-u—but it's spelled e-w-e. It's a female sheep."

"Can I see her?" Chess asked. "Would that be okay?"

Joni shrugged. "Sure!" She led the way downstairs.

In one of the small wooden pens, a lone ewe stood facing toward the back pasture, bleating loudly. "Why is she roaring like that?" Chess asked. "Is she in pain?"

"Sheep don't like being by themselves." To stop the noise, Joni grabbed a weed from outside the door. The moment she saw it, the sheep forgot her friends. She scarfed the weed down with a gasping, gobbling sound, and Chess chuckled, the Archie-eating-carrots laugh.

"That's great! Can I give her one?" And they were back to easy again. The ewe ate weed after weed, and her swift lips and glassy, demented-looking yellow eyes never seemed to get less funny.

"What's her name?" Chess asked. "I can't just call her 'Hey, ewe!'"

"Good one!" Joni said. "She doesn't actually have a name."

"She doesn't have a *name*?"

"There's a hundred and fifty of them! Even Dad can't tell them apart. They have numbers, see?" Joni pointed to the metal tag clipped into the sheep's ear.

Chess looked suddenly sober. "That must hurt."

"Like getting your ears pierced." Joni had gotten hers done last year, but she didn't wear earrings enough and the holes grew shut again.

"I have pierced ears," Chess said. "But I decided to. The ewe didn't *want* her ear pierced!"

"Sheep don't want anything, except to eat," Joni said. "This one wants another weed."

She plucked one and the sheep inhaled it, but Chess didn't laugh this time. "Do you *shear* your sheep?" she asked in a troubled voice.

"Of course!" Joni said. "Otherwise, they'd have wool out to *here*!"

"But it's cruel!"

"Shearing isn't cruel!" Joni said. "It's a *haircut*!"

Chess whipped out her phone. *Tap tap tap.* "That's a *haircut*?" She turned the phone to Joni. It showed a photo of a sheep with almost no wool on its body. Its belly and sides were dark red with blood and scabs.

"That's not what shearing looks like!" Joni said.

"They don't get cut?" Chess asked.

"No! Well, sometimes, but—just little nicks, once in a while, and they heal really fast."

"So that *never* happens?"

Joni made herself look at the picture. It was a photograph, so it was real. It must have happened to *that* sheep. "No," she said. Her voice felt weak. "No," she repeated more strongly. "Or we wouldn't do it!"

Chess said, "People should wear cotton, not wool! Let's give this ewe some more weeds. She's obviously hungry. Or does food make *sheep* sick, too?"

Something in Joni's chest went thin and papery, like a hornets' nest with the hornets about to come boiling out. Chess did *not* know her well enough to get sarcastic!

But before she could think of what to say, Tobin popped his head through the door. "Hey, Joni, the sheep on that back meadow are out. Do you know where your dad is?"

"Making cheese," Joni said. "I'll get him." She took off running, not even looking back to see what Chess did. Because who cared? Really, who cared?

White rubber boots were lined up beside the door of the cheese house. Joni slipped on a pair and walked inside. Olivia was dipping curds out of a vat and packing them into a strainer. Dad pressed on them to squeeze out the whey, and Rosita watched. The whole room smelled sweet and milky and clean.

"Sheep are out," Joni said.

"You ready to take over?" Dad asked Rosita. She nodded, and he walked out with Joni, back across the driveway to Tobin, Chess, and the truck. "Who wants to ride along?" He whistled for the dogs.

Joni didn't. She'd had enough of the Chess/sheep combination. "There's no room," she started to say, but Tobin hopped up in the back and reached his hand down to her. "Come on, Joni, there's plenty of room." In a moment, they were all packed into the back of the pickup with the border collies. The truck bounced across the grass. The dogs hung their heads over the sides, looking toward the sheep.

"Is that safe?" Chess asked. "What if they jump out?"

"They won't!" Joni said. No dog on this farm had ever jumped out of the truck and hurt itself. But Chess believed the worst about everything.

Tobin said, "Don't worry. These dogs are smart. The only reason they aren't driving is that they can't work the clutch!"

That brought a thin smile to Chess's face, but she still kept an eye on Millie and Zip. They began to tremble when they saw the sheep, spread across the back field and eating fast as if to make the most of their stolen time. Dad stopped the truck and got out. *"Wait!"* he told the dogs.

He and Tobin went to disconnect the electricity and fix the fence. The dogs stood in the pickup bed, staring intently at the sheep. Millie shivered; Zip whined. Chess stroked them, but they paid no attention.

Across the field, Dad called. "Millie, Zip! Come by!" The dogs rocketed over the side of the truck and streaked across the grass. The sheep flung their heads up. Bunched together, swirling and baaing, they wheeled toward the opening in the fence. Dad whistled, and the dogs flattened on their bellies as the sheep streamed between them into the pasture, all bleating loudly.

Chess said, "The dogs love it, don't they?"

"More than anything!" Joni said.

"How do the *sheep* feel?"

Heat flashed over Joni from head to toe. "I don't *know* how the sheep feel! Sheep are—"

"No," Chess said, half-turning toward Joni. "I didn't mean—I want to *understand*. I thought the sheep would be really stressed out. Like, terrified! They're being chased by dogs! And I don't know anything about sheep, maybe I'm wrong . . . but they don't *look* stressed. Are they?"

Maybe I'm wrong? Had Joni heard that right? "They went right back to eating," she said. "How stressed can they be?"

"So why do they run?" Chess asked. "Because—I mean, it almost looks like a game."

"Yes." But that sounded like she was mad. Joni tried again. "It's kind of like—the dogs agree to chase and the sheep agree to run. But there's one old sheep that *won't* run. She butts the dogs when they try to make her. They hate that! Dad does, too. It messes everything up."

Chess chuckled. "I'd like to meet *that* sheep!"

And things were easy again! But this was hard work. Joni was ready for a break. "Actually, even that sheep is pretty boring. Can we do something at your house tomorrow?"

"But . . ." Chess hesitated. "Sure. We could do that."

SIXTEEN

Baling Twine

Chess stayed till almost lunchtime. In the afternoon, Joni rode Archie over to Danae's. Alyssa was there, and already it was starting to be like last summer. Danae would begin a sentence and Alyssa would finish it and Joni wouldn't understand. Like when Danae said "I think we should—" and Alyssa said "go fishing!" and they both laughed. After that, "go fishing" was the end of every sentence, and they couldn't explain because they were laughing too hard. "Go fishing" had happened since yesterday.

At least Danae was interested in last night's riding lesson, and Joni was able to show off. The head-turning technique didn't work as well without someone to mold her into the shape of a perfect rider. But when Joni pretended she was Mrs. Abernathy, she was able to turn Archie with a lot less effort than normal.

Danae wanted to try it, too. She got Pumpkin out, and Joni tried to explain how Mrs. Abernathy had aligned her. There were too many words, though, too many details. "Pretend you're that plastic cowboy that goes with the gray model horse," she said at last. The cowboy sort of plugged into the horse's saddle. Pretending to be him, Danae looked plugged in as well. But Pumpkin still wouldn't do the magic turn.

"Pretend you're—" But Danae didn't know Mrs. Abernathy. "Pretend you're a queen!" Joni said.

Danae's chin came up. Her face looked stern, she turned her head commandingly, and Pumpkin turned, too, as if the two of them were one. Danae pumped her fist. "We are going to *rock* 4-H camp! I can't wait!"

That was a good visit. But all the way home, the image of that scabby sheep kept coming back to Joni. She couldn't *not* see it, and it made a spot in her chest feel bad, like it had gone rotten.

Dad was mowing hay, and Olivia, Tobin, and Rosita were going swimming. They asked Joni to go with them, but she was sick of being the little kid in the middle of their conversation. Instead, she helped Mom spiff up the farm store.

Mom had painted the inside last weekend, a creamy, cheesy white. Joni helped her hang the blue-and-white-checked curtains and spread a cloth on the sample table. She filled a basket with plump skeins of yarn—*People should wear cotton, not wool!*—while Mom slipped the new *Boston Globe* article into a frame.

Then she got out Dad's grazing journal and opened it to the right page. It told where the sheep had been grazing when today's cheese was made, and what plants they were eating. Dad's journals were what got Mom interested in him in the first place. Reading about clover and mint, and finding hints of them in the cheese, she fell in love, as she always did, with good writing. Anyway, that was what she'd told Joni, who obviously wasn't around back then. That was right after he got divorced, when he was lonely and had time to write extra-long entries in his pasture journals.

Joni dusted and straightened the pictures on the wall—A very young Dad proudly displayed one of his first cheeses. The caption read, "Not As Good As It Looks!"

The picture of Dad in France, with three old men in black berets, was captioned, "It Gets Better." Kate and Olivia, around Joni's age, held a Cheese Society blue ribbon and plaque; Dad handed a slice of cheese to Julia Child; Dad held baby Joni in one arm and a large cheese in the other, with a big bronze medal on it. And there were half a dozen photos of contented sheep, pictures beautiful enough to go on a magazine cover.

No pictures of shearing, though.

But there could *be,* Joni thought. Shearing was pretty enough even for a store picture. Joni loved to see Dad peel back the dingy gray outer wool, showing the clean wool underneath. It was creamy white like the walls of the store, soft and wavy with a strong smell of sheep, and no blood, ever. Once in a while, Dad accidentally made a tiny nick in a sheep's skin, but the blood didn't even trickle—

Joni squeezed her eyes shut, but that scabby sheep was

inside her head. She couldn't close it out, and when she opened her eyes, Mom was looking at her. "What's wrong?"

Joni told her about the picture. "Why would that happen?" she asked. "I mean—that never happens!"

"I can't imagine," Mom said. "Shearing a sheep isn't hard—I've done it! I'll bet it's propaganda, Joni. Do you know what propaganda is?" Joni shook her head. "It's misinformation, or half-truths, designed to sway people's emotions. Propaganda tries to make you so mad or scared that you don't think. You just react, without pausing to ask yourself, 'How do I know that's true?'"

Joni said, "It was a photograph."

"Photographs can be altered easily," Mom said. "And you know, give me a can of dark red spray paint and I could make a scabby sheep for you! So I don't know if the sheep was really hurt. But the point is, neither do you, and neither does your friend Chess."

"I wish we were shearing now," Joni said. "Then she'd see."

Mom said, "She'll learn soon enough. I'm glad there's another girl in the neighborhood. It will be nice for you to have a friend so close." Mom totally understood the Danae and Alyssa thing.

As they arranged the jelly jars, a car pulled into the parking area. A moment later, Chess's mother opened the door. "Oh, hello! I'm just—I didn't think you staffed the store."

"Usually, it's self-service," Mom said, "but here we are!" She explained that eggs and cheese were in the refrigerator, along with cheese samples.

"They're vegans," Joni said quickly.

Mrs. Ventura shook her head. "No. Well, we have been, but not anymore. Not all of us, and I'd love to sample your cheese."

She opened the refrigerator and fumbled with the glass covers and the toothpicks. Was this the actual moment she was stopping being vegan? Joni pretended not to watch as a piece of cheese went into Mrs. Ventura's mouth. Her eyes closed.

"Oh, my goodness," she said. "Delicious! I haven't had a piece of cheese in four years. And this one is part cow's milk?"

She tried them both, she loved them both, and she ended up buying a wedge of each, along with a dozen eggs. Mom showed her the sturdy wooden cashbox. It had a slot in the top to put money through, and the lid was padlocked shut.

"So, really, you just leave it out here?"

"It's built into the counter," Mom said. "You'd need a chain saw to steal it!"

"Amazing!"

"How are you liking Vermont?" Mom asked.

Mrs. Ventura made a vague gesture. "Everything's so different. The green. The . . . the smallness. Very beautiful. That's why I'm going vegetarian. I see how rich this land is, and it makes me hungry. I can't eat grass and I'm still not ready to eat meat, but I'm ready to try this."

"That's . . . good," Mom said.

"Also," Mrs. Ventura said, "I know your animals are treated ethically. I can see it, and I know your family. So that makes me feel like maybe this could be okay."

It was almost an insult, and anyway, how could Mrs. Ventura judge how the animals were treated? She probably didn't know any more than Chess did! But Joni could tell Mrs. Ventura didn't mean it that way. She sounded tentative and fragile, and Joni felt sorry for her. She would have to take these eggs and those wedges of cheese home to Chess. What would that be like?

"Everybody loves our cheese," Joni said. "Did you read the pasture journal for that day? The sheep grazed in the pasture with the wild garlic."

"Wild garlic!" Mrs. Ventura whispered. Mom's eyebrows popped up.

"Since when did you become such a saleswoman?" she asked when Chess's mother had closed the door behind her. "We may have to send you to the Farmers' Market this year!"

The door reopened, and Mrs. Ventura poked her head back in. "I almost forgot—Chess wanted me to pick something up for her. A pile of twine? She said you'd know, Joni."

Joni got in the car with her and rode along to the barn. Mrs. Ventura bent tensely over the wheel, watching the swirl of dogs. Why was she so nerved up? She didn't seem like the kind of person who would have a daughter like Chess.

She walked into the barn and stopped in her tracks, looking up at the swallows, and the light streaming through every crack in the boards. "Oh, my! This is amazing. And I understand you have kittens?"

"They're not out here anymore," Joni said. "We took them into the house." Mrs. Ventura's face fell. She was a total cat person, Joni realized. Just like Chess. *We don't believe in keeping captive animals.* Who was "we"?

"Here's the baling twine." She scooped up a huge armful. "Where should I put it?"

Mrs. Ventura opened the side door. "On the floor, I guess.

It's got a lot of old grass in it, doesn't it?"

"Hay," Joni said. "That's hay."

"Yes, of course," Mrs. Ventura said. "Hay. I don't know what anything is here. I feel like a complete idiot. Did you ever move, Joni?"

"No." Joni couldn't imagine living anywhere else. She dumped the heap of baling twine onto the floor of the van.

"Thank you," Mrs. Ventura said. "I wonder what she's going to do with it!"

SEVENTEEN

A T-Shirt

In the morning, Joni headed over to Chess's house on Archie. It was a perfect day for a ride, cool and misty. And a perfect place to ride, through fields and woods to visit a friend.

A friend? Yes, Joni decided. For every downturn, every moment of discomfort, there had been an upturn, usually involving feeding an animal and laughing. She could handle ups and downs, right?

Chess was waiting for her out by the barn. "Do you want to put him inside, or out in the pen?"

The pen was a paddock at the side of the barn, knee-high with lush grass. "Inside," Joni said. "That's too much feed for him."

"He could have a little," Chess said. "Couldn't he?" Archie

was gazing at the paddock with his ears pricked, looking pretty and soulful.

"Okay, ten minutes," Joni said. She released him in the paddock, and they leaned on the fence to watch him graze. Chess didn't speak. She was pale today and kept nibbling her lips.

But maybe she just wanted to watch Archie, who was having a wonderful time tearing off mouthfuls of grass with a happy, juicy, ripping sound. It was nice to be with somebody who didn't think that was boring. "I wish I could eat grass," Joni said. "It must be like baling into a huge plate of spaghetti!"

"He seems hungry," Chess said.

"He's a pony," Joni said. "They're always hungry! How long has it been?"

Chess shrugged. "Five minutes?"

"No, really. Can you check your phone?"

Chess looked away so Joni couldn't see her face. "I don't have it anymore."

"Did you lose it?" That was one reason Mom and Dad wouldn't let Joni have one. She wasn't great at keeping track of things.

"I didn't lose it," Chess said. "They took it away."

"Oh. Sorry." Now Joni saw that Chess's eyes were red. Should she ask what had happened? Because Chess had her phone yesterday. But maybe she'd better not go there. It seemed like a big deal, and they weren't that kind of friends yet. "Anyway, I'm going to put him in now."

"Already?"

Joni said, "There are two kinds of ponies, our vet says. Those that *have* foundered, and those that *will* founder. Archie's an easy keeper. He gets fat just looking at grass."

Chess's dark eyes were large and serious. "So he can't *ever* eat as much as he wants?"

"He can eat as much *hay* as he wants," Joni said. She knew what that meant. Hay was like spinach. Grass was like chocolate cake. But it was necessary. "Foundering is horrible. It can be so bad, you can never ride them again."

Chess folded her lips and didn't say anything. *She thinks it's all about riding,* Joni realized. *She thinks it's all about me.* Now would be the time, if *she* had a phone, to pull it out and show Chess a picture of Hooper, and a diagram of a foundered hoof. But Chess would understand as soon as Joni took her to Kalysta's. Meanwhile, this would be a good time to change the subject, if Joni could think of anything to say.

She looked off across the Venturas' broad fields. Someone had walked out there recently, treading a path through the tall grass. They'd dropped a piece of baling twine. "How's your twine project?"

"Secret," Chess said.

Joni felt her cheeks get hot. Okay, this was worse than "go fishing"! Why did it have to be so hard? She went in to catch Archie, but he twisted away from her and trotted around the paddock, snatching bites of grass. Joni heard laughter, sharp and mean sounding.

"Come *help* me!"

"Why?" Chess asked. "Why should he always have to do what you want?"

"Right *now* so he doesn't make himself sick! So help!"

"He's your slave, you catch him!" Chess said. "Go, Archie!"

Joni gritted her teeth and charged after Archie, trapping him in a corner of the paddock. He whirled and Joni stepped straight into his path. She could get hurt if he ran over her. She was too mad to care.

But Archie never carried a game too far. He stopped, pricking his ears innocently, and Chess chuckled, that deep, rich laugh that had first made Joni like her, not the sharp laughter of a few moments ago. "He's so cute! 'Who, *me*?'"

Working fast, Joni slipped on the hackamore. Archie ducked his head and nuzzled her arm, his dark eyes wide and soft. "You're a *brat*!" she told him, leading him into the barn.

It had a broad aisle and four large, sturdy box stalls. Two were stacked with lumber, electric fence wire, and a few fiberglass posts from the last time horses had lived here, but the stall nearest the door was empty. Joni put Archie in it and tested the automatic waterer. It didn't work.

"Do you have a bucket?"

"I don't know," Chess said.

Joni found a clean bucket in one of the storage stalls, filled it at the outside tap, and lugged it to Archie's stall. "Can I borrow back a piece of baling twine?"

"I don't have any here," Chess said.

"Oh. Okay, I saw a piece out behind the barn," Joni said. "I'll go grab that."

The baling twine was farther out in the field than she remembered. She picked it up and looked along the path of trampled grass toward the back fields. This would be an *incredible* place for horses. If Kalysta had this much land . . . maybe she should bring up the rescue idea again, when Chess settled into being nice. She must be upset about the phone, and whatever had happened to make her parents take it away.

Chess was in with Archie when Joni got back, trying to stroke his neck. He ignored her, checking out the stall for hidden sources of food. "Scratch his shoulder," Joni said. "That's what he likes."

Chess raked Archie's shoulder with her nails. He turned his head toward her, bright-eyed, suddenly interested. After a moment, his silver-velvet muzzle started to scrub on her shoulder.

"What's he *doing*?" Chess sounded scared, but she didn't flinch.

"Scratching you back," Joni said. "Horses do that with each other. The harder you scratch, the harder he'll scratch, so be careful."

Chess reached up with her other hand and scratched more vigorously, laughing as Archie rasped her with his lip. Joni saw his teeth flash. "Watch out!"

"*Ow!*" Chess jumped back, rubbing her shoulder.

"You okay?" Joni asked. "They kind of nip each other when they scratch shoulders."

Chess said, "Next time, I'll wear a coat!"

Joni tied the bucket to the automatic waterer so it couldn't tip, just in time. Archie reached over her shoulder, shoved in his muzzle, and gave a vigorous slosh. When the pail didn't tip, he went on exploring the stall.

"So, what do you want to do?" Chess asked. "Go watch the miniature horses?"

That was progress. She didn't call them ponies this time. "Watch them do what?" Joni asked.

"Just watch them. I take binoculars and a notebook. I'm documenting what's going on over there."

"What do you mean, what's going on?" Joni asked, though she had a feeling she didn't want to hear the answer.

Chess pulled a small notebook out of her back pocket and flipped it open. "Okay, yesterday? Two whole hours tied to the fence, wearing all those straps. And see?" She turned the page, showing a set of hash marks. "Every *single* day they wear those muzzles! They never get a chance to eat freely. Why shouldn't they get at least a half hour to eat as much as they want? You do that for Archie!"

"Maybe they do get a chance," Joni said.

"No. I've gone up there fifteen times in the last four days and they *never* had the muzzles off!"

"They must need them," Joni said. "'Cause Mrs. Abernathy knows all about horses. Anyway, if she takes them off, maybe she wouldn't be able to catch the minis to put them back on. She has a bad hip—"

"People who can't take care of animals shouldn't have them," Chess said.

Who gets to decide? Joni felt a chill in her stomach. She said, "Well, it doesn't hurt them to stand tied. They were probably just going to stand around, anyway."

Chess looked straight at Joni for a moment, head tipped to one side. "Okay. We won't go." She hesitated. "Look—you're nice, Joni. I think we can be friends. But you know what? There are things we'd better not talk about, okay?"

Okay? How could that be okay? How could they be friends if they couldn't talk about everything? Joni didn't know what "go fishing" meant, but she knew she could break into whatever that was all about, and Danae and Alyssa would abandon the game and listen to her. And "you're *nice*, Joni"? That was practically an insult! Did she need a friend this badly?

No. But she wanted one. She wanted *Chess*. Because—that laugh. The flashes of complete understanding and ease. And the challenge. She liked that, at least some of the time. Anyway, she was Joni; she wasn't somebody who quarreled with people . . .

"Okay," she said, looking down.

"Good," Chess said. "Come on—we'll chill out in my room for a while."

Joni had never been inside the white house. It was big, old, and expensive-looking, with elegant pale-colored furniture and real paintings on the walls. It smelled of lemon-scented cleaner, and there was a large cardboard mover's box in the middle of the kitchen. *Fun for cats*, Joni thought, automatically looking around for one—but, no, no cats here.

Chess's mother stood on a stool, arranging dishes on a shelf. "Hi, Joni!" she said. "Your brother's napping, Francesca. If you're quiet, he shouldn't bother you."

Chess led Joni through the house. The dining room and living room also had boxes in them, but Chess's room looked as if it had been hers for years. There were posters of celebrities on all the walls—at least, they had to be celebrities, because what other people had posters made of them? Joni didn't know who they were, but they were all posing with animals—dogs, cats, a horse, a lion.

But there were no real animals in the house. Joni realized she was listening for the sound of a cat's paws hitting the floor as it jumped down from a high place, or the jingle of tags on a dog's collar. At most houses she'd been in, there would eventually be a sound like that. Not here.

She sat down on the tightly made bed, and then she saw it— the same picture she'd seen on Olivia's phone. The photo had been cropped so the dog crate didn't show, and you couldn't tell that the red jacket was actually a ringmaster's coat. All you could see was Chess's grandmother's face.

It was a nice picture, actually. She was a young-looking grandmother, with dark, short hair cut almost exactly the way Chess's was, and very bright eyes. She looked happy and proud. Joni was glad to see a real person, someone she could ask a question about. "Who is this?"

"Nana. My grandmother." Chess didn't seem to want to say more, and Joni felt a prickle of anger. One more thing they weren't supposed to talk about? Well, so what! She was sick of being bossed around!

"Is she your mom's mom?" She made her voice pleasant, like a persistent pest of a kid who didn't pick up on subtle signals. And she waited.

"Yes," Chess said. For a second, it seemed like she wasn't going to say more, but then she went on. "Mom had to stay in bed for five months when she was pregnant with Noah, so Nana moved in with us. Then he was sick, so she stayed."

"Is she going to come live here?" That could be bad—the

ringmaster grandmother next door to the farm.

Chess looked away. "She has her life. She was with us for four whole years. So . . ."

Joni didn't ask, "Do you miss her?" That was obvious—and she knew how it felt. She still missed Grandpa sometimes, and he died when she was eight. "Maybe you can go back and spend part of the summer with her."

Chess glanced away again. Then she looked straight at Joni. "Do you *like* that shirt?"

"*What?*" Joni looked down at herself. What was she even wearing? A blue T-shirt, from some political campaign. It had a guy's name in big letters across the chest. "No," she said. "It's just a shirt."

"I can show you how to fix it so it will actually look good," Chess said. "It's easy." She opened the drawer in her bedside table and took out a large pair of scissors.

"You're going to cut it? Where?" What would Mom think?

"Take it off," Chess said.

Really? Take off her shirt? But Joni was too curious not to.

Chess sat cross-legged on the bed and bent over the shirt. Carefully, she cut along the neckband. *Snick snick snick.* The scissors parted the band from the rest of the shirt, and it fell to the floor like a fat blue caterpillar.

"Put it back on," Chess said. Joni obeyed and stood up to look for a mirror.

"Hold still." Chess went down on one knee, frowning. After a second, she started snipping again. In a moment, the whole bottom section of the shirt fell around Joni's feet.

"Now hold your arms out," Chess said. *Snick snick*—part

of one sleeve slid down to Joni's wrist. Chess walked around behind her and did the other one.

"Now." She opened her closet door, and Joni saw herself in the full-length mirror.

"Wow!" The shirt was short, stopping just above the waistband of her jeans in an arching line. The sleeves were light and fluttery. With the neckband gone, the thin material lay close to Joni's body, letting the little hollows at the base of her neck show. It was pretty. *She* was pretty.

"Where did you learn to do that?"

"Nana," Chess said.

"Wow. That's cool!"

"*She's* cool," Chess said. "She makes the world better every day."

Her voice sounded shaky all of a sudden. Joni saw tears in her eyes. It must be horrible to move all the way across the country from someone you love. "She sure made this shirt better! Tell her thank you."

The tears released down Chess's face. "They won't let me talk to her."

EIGHTEEN

"How *We* Eat the Grass"

"Why?" Joni asked. Not letting someone talk to their grandmother was huge!

"They snooped around in my stuff." Chess squeezed her eyes shut, shaking her head. "They think she's still too much of an influence."

So that *was* why they moved! Another thing Joni couldn't say. She made a sympathetic noise.

Chess rubbed away her tears with the snipped-off end of one of Joni's sleeves. "But we're not stopping. This is a campaign, like antislavery. It might take a long time, but we're going to end this!"

It all spilled out, Chess talking rapidly now as if to make up for how quiet she'd been before. Cows—the whole world overheating because people eat meat, and cow farts contain methane that causes global warming, and there wouldn't *be* cows if people didn't eat meat and drink milk. And eggs—chickens packed in cages so they couldn't even move, just because people wanted to eat eggs.

"We're going to get carriage horses out of cities, too," Chess said. "We're going to set them free. Nana just helped a whole bunch of ponies that were being forced to give rides. The police took them away from the owner and they're going to be retired—"

"Retired *where*?" Joni asked. Her voice came out loud, rudely loud, and she didn't care. "*Where* will the ponies go?"

"I don't know," Chess said, blinking. "Probably a shelter—"

"No," Joni said. "Shelters for horses are usually full."

"You don't know that," Chess said. "This was California—"

"It's expensive to keep horses," Joni said. "Everywhere! That's why they need to have jobs, like those ponies did. Do you know what happens to horses that don't have jobs? They get sold by the pound! For meat!"

Chess's face went pale. But after a moment, she lifted her chin. "Maybe that's better than a life of misery."

"And maybe it's *not*!" Joni said. Her voice just came out of her. She didn't have to think. "Because, pony-ride ponies? They're usually not good at anything else! They're old and slow and plain, but they're gentle, and they have a job, and it's *easy*! All they have to do is walk. Maybe it doesn't look exciting, but it beats being dead!"

Chess stared stubbornly back at her, lips firmly pressed together.

Suddenly, Joni wanted Archie. She wanted to see him, touch him, hug him. She wanted to mount up and ride away, as fast as she could.

"I've got to go," she said, and as soon as it came out, she knew what she was really saying.

Chess did, too. She hesitated, then asked, "Can I still come see the kittens?"

"Why do you even want to?" Joni asked.

Chess made a sound like a hiccup. "Because they're kittens! I can't help it!"

"I don't know," Joni said. "Call me in a couple of days."

She walked down the stairs. Chess followed. Joni didn't know why, because this was over. There was no point in even being polite about it.

"Leaving already?" Mrs. Ventura asked as they passed through the kitchen. "I was going to make cookies."

"That's okay," Joni said. "Thanks."

They went out to the barn. Archie nickered when he saw them, thrusting his head over the stall door. Joni didn't hug him, not with Chess there. She saddled up, led him out, and mounted.

"'Bye," Chess said. She looked small and her face was smudged, but Joni didn't feel sorry for her. Without a word, she turned Archie toward the bridge and let him trot, and when she reached the brook trail, she let him gallop.

She clattered up into the farmyard, which was full of activity. Olivia and Rosita were talking in the cheese house. Tobin drove the tractor toward the upper hayfield, pulling the rake. The Bears woofed in friendly greeting. The border collies waited in the back of the truck for Dad, and the mother cat waited at the door of the house with a mouse in her jaws.

Chess wanted to end all this. She didn't understand keeping animals, she thought it was slavery, and they couldn't be friends, not ever. And that might not be the worst of it. Would they have Chess in a dog crate someday, out in front of the milking parlor?

Joni stripped off Archie's tack, rubbed him down, and gave him carrots, as he demanded. Now, finally, she could hug his neck. He jerked his head up when her arms went around him, making it difficult, but Joni hung on, pressing her face against his springy mane and breathing him in. With an annoyed sigh, he stopped trying to shrug her off and let her lean there.

The usual peace didn't come. Joni felt angry, and proud of herself. She'd spoken up, finally. She really had. But she also felt as if she'd broken something valuable, and no one knew it yet.

She turned Archie loose and went outside. This was one of the times when the border collies only imagined Dad was going to take them somewhere. Really, he was leaning into the depths of the baler. It was a cranky old piece of machinery that liked to make alarming sounds and grind to a halt when there was a lot of hay to get in.

"Is it broken?" Joni asked.

"Not yet." Dad looked up. "Hey, what's wrong?"

Joni didn't know how to say it. Finally, she just said, "Chess."

"The animal rights thing? Olivia showed us that picture," Dad explained.

Joni nodded. "Are we—is it—why is it okay? That we raise sheep and eat them?"

Dad leaned against the baler, crossing his arms. "Why is it

okay?" he repeated thoughtfully. "Well, it's our nature. We're one of the animals that eats other animals, like the wolves and lions."

"And that's okay?" Joni asked. "That we're lions?"

"Well, unlike the lions, we actually take care of the sheep," Dad said. "And it's not *all* okay. That's why we don't buy eggs from chickens kept in tiny cages, or meat from cattle kept in feedlots. I give my own animals a life that's as close to nature as I can make it. I owe them that. It's part of the deal."

"But we don't *have* to eat meat," Joni said. "We could stop, right?" Why was she pushing this? She wasn't Chess, and she wasn't Chess's friend, so why did she have to win Chess's argument? Still, it seemed important.

Dad said, "I need the sheep to have lambs so I have milk for cheese making. I can't keep them all, so some get eaten. Sure, I could stop making cheese, Joni. I could get rid of the sheep. But this is the way I've figured out to make a living on this farm, and to build the soil. The way we graze our sheep puts carbon back into the ground. It cools the planet, and it makes great cheese. I think it's ethical. More than ethical—for me, it's practically holy! But I'm aware that I could be wrong. It's all a great mystery. Why we're here on earth. What we're for."

He paused, waiting for Joni to say something. But what was there to say?

"All I know is, I bow my head," Dad said. "I ask to be guided. I honor the animals—their nature and their sacrifice. I thank them for the life they've let me make. You're free to choose a different life, Joni, if that seems right to you."

Joni nodded. It seemed impossible to speak. She didn't know

what seemed right anymore, and she didn't want a different life, and her heart felt too large for her chest, smothering her.

"Hey," Dad said. "Want a hug? 'Cause I sure do!"

Joni went to lean into his arms. She heard the scrabble of claws as the border collies launched from the back of the pickup. A moment later, two jealous sharp-nosed heads pushed in between her legs and Dad's. Dad smelled like sheep and sunshine, and a little bit like tractor grease. She rested her cheek on his T-shirt and sighed, and didn't cry after all, though she still felt the hard lump in her chest. "I can't wait for camp."

"This friendship's pretty complicated, isn't it?"

"We're not friends," Joni said.

"I'm sorry." Dad rubbed the back of her head with one hand, patting dogs with the other, and they all stood together for several minutes. Dad didn't talk, or try to make it okay, and Joni was grateful for that.

And she was grateful to have a bedroom full of kittens to spend the rest of the morning with, and a table full of people to eat lunch with. Grandma DeeDee dropping by. Customers at the cheese shop. Joni was glad to see them all. This wasn't a day to be alone.

In the afternoon, she helped get in the hay, after changing out of her redesigned T-shirt. She still liked *it*, anyway. Dad drove one tractor around the field with the baler chugging behind him, spitting out a bale every couple of minutes. Olivia drove the other tractor, pulling the wagon. When she came to a heap of bales, she stopped, and she and Tobin put them on the wagon. Joni wasn't strong enough to lift them that high, so she and Rosita got on the wagon and stacked.

The first bale took all of Joni's strength, even with Rosita's help. How could she pick up the next one? But she did, and then another, and another, until she stopped wondering. Of course she could. The rough grass stems prickled her arms, and the baling twine hurt her hands. When Olivia noticed that, she pulled off her gloves and tossed them up. They were too big, but they helped. The bales built up higher and higher, until Joni and Rosita were riding on a castle that moved slowly across the hilltop, almost bumping the clouds. A sweet, dry scent surrounded them, and a haze of sunlit dust.

From her great height, Joni looked down on Olivia and Tobin. They moved easily together, working hard, but there was a kind of zing between them. Joni hadn't seen them kissing or holding hands yet, but she was sure that was in the works.

"That's turning into a great romance!" Rosita said dryly.

"I guess so."

"Not the summer you hoped for, is it?" Rosita said. "Me, either, actually. I was going to spend it with my best bud—but, hey! I introduced them."

"He's nice, right?" Joni asked.

"I've known him since we were in fourth grade," Rosita said. "He's nice to the bone, and smart—everything you could hope for in a best friend's boyfriend!" She laughed in a sort of sad way, and Joni wondered if Rosita wished Tobin had fallen in love with her. Or maybe she just wanted a sliver of Olivia's attention. Good luck with that!

They filled two huge wagons, and that was all of the hay for today. Dad backed the wagons into the barn. "We'll unload them tomorrow," he said. "Let's wash up and eat!"

This was the first time Joni had really helped get hay in, not just ridden on the wagon. She was surprised at how good she felt. Like Mrs. Abernathy said—she'd spent hours in the heat, lifting bales that were too heavy for her over and over and over again, but she was still standing upright. She felt tired and itchy and starved, but strong.

Half an hour later, freshly showered, everyone gathered at the picnic table. Mom lit candles, though it was still light out. "On your menu this evening," she said, setting a huge lasagna pan down. "Garden salad, fresh peas, and mac and cheese made with our own cheese."

Dad reached for the serving spoon and ladled a huge scoop of mac and cheese onto Tobin's plate. He said, "This is how *we* eat the grass."

NINETEEN

Wave. Say Hi.

Joni woke the next morning with kittens draped all over her, and the mother cat lying on her chest. Something had seeped into her body from theirs, and she felt as relaxed as they were. She lay there watching how her breath lifted and dropped them. How nice it must be to lie on top of a large, trusted, breathing creature. What if the earth breathed?

Then she thought of Chess and her breath stopped lifting them so high.

She eased out from under the kittens and got dressed, putting on the T-shirt Chess had fixed yesterday. At least she'd learned how to do that!

Mom was sitting at the kitchen table with her long hair down her back and her beautiful leather-bound notebook in front of her. Joni fixed a bowl of cereal with milk and strawberries and sat down across from her. Mom's pen kept going for a few moments, then hesitated, then stopped. She looked up.

"You okay, Joni?"

Dad must have told her about Chess. Joni shrugged, with her mouth full.

"Well, here's how things are going for me!" Mom said. "The summer quiet that I wanted very badly has been filled up with serious young people talking about soil carbon and rotational grazing. The family I cook for has doubled in size. So I've decided to go on a writing retreat for a couple of days."

"Will you be back before I go to camp?"

"Yes, I'll come see you off. But you'd better start packing, Joni. I don't want it to be like last year."

Joni laughed. "I forgot my girth, remember?"

"I don't remember it being funny at the time," Mom said. "So—apparently, Rosita can cook. You can show her where things are. Your dad knows how to reach me, but I'm sure that won't be necessary. Olivia's going to keep the farm store stocked. Still, check on that, Joni, will you? You're more familiar with it than she is. Is that all okay?"

It had to be okay, and of course Joni said it was. Mom looked at her skeptically, then kissed her own fingers and reached across the table to press them on Joni's forehead. "I'm sorry, Jon-Jon. I'm just really hungry for some peace and quiet."

"A lot of people would laugh at that," Joni said.

"A lot of people don't actually live on farms!" Mom said.

Joni walked her out to her car. As Mom put her laptop in the trunk, Danae's mother drove in and pulled up beside the farm store. Danae and Alyssa got out. "Mom needs eggs," Danae said, "and we need kittens!"

"Okay," Joni said. She hugged Mom goodbye and turned to them.

Alyssa was looking at Joni's T-shirt. "Wow, did you do that?"

"Chess did," Joni said, leading the way to her bedroom.

"Cool! I'm totally getting her to show me."

Joni made herself say, "Okay, but—I'm not friends with her anymore."

She shut the door quickly as kittens surged toward it. For once, they weren't the center of attention. "Talk," Danae said.

"She's crazy into animal rescue," Joni said.

"Well—*we're* into animal rescue," Alyssa said. She wasn't in 4-H, but she came to Kalysta's sometimes.

Joni shook her head, picking up a random kitten to cuddle against her cheek. "Yesterday? She told me her grandmother got these poor pony-ride ponies taken away from their owner and . . . I mean, they probably *died*! And when I told her that, she said maybe they were better off dead!"

Danae's eyes widened. Alyssa said, *"Intense!"* Which was funny. Of the three of them, Alyssa was the intense one. But it was true. Chess was way, way too intense.

"But I still have to ride by her house," Joni said. "What do I say?"

"Don't go that way," Danae said.

"No," Alyssa said. "Joni needs to be able to ride wherever she wants. Besides—Chess will be in our class. She'll ride on our bus—like, forever! So we need to deal. Anyway, you don't hate her, Joni, right?"

"No, I . . . like her. Sometimes."

"So just ride by the house and wave," Alyssa said. "Or . . . maybe she wants to come see the kittens?"

"She does," Joni said. "She has been."

"If she asks to come over, call us," Alyssa said. "We'll come down. It's easier if there's more people. We can all be friendly without being *friends*-friends—and if we're watching kittens, we won't have to talk about anything else!"

Kittens were no guarantee with Chess, but Joni felt better. Smile. Wave. Call her friends. It sounded doable. "You guys are the best!"

"Oh, yes!" Danae said. "We have certificates and everything!"

After they left, Joni picked a fresh bouquet of red clover and buttercups for the store. She was cutting more cheese samples when Mrs. Abernathy came in. "I was hoping I'd see you! How's the riding? Did the lesson hold?"

Joni hesitated. "Kind of."

"You should have one more before camp," Mrs. Abernathy said. "Can you come over this morning? We'll use my back field. It's flat and shady."

So right away she'd have to ride past Chess's house. "Could we do it here?" Joni wanted to suggest. But, no, she had a plan. Wave. Say hi. "Okay," she said.

"Good. See you around te—no, today's Wednesday, isn't it? Wednesday mornings are dedicated to the chiropractor. How about three thirty?"

"Okay," Joni said. "See you then!"

In the house, she checked for phone messages. "A couple of days," she'd told Chess, but she was pretty sure Chess would want to see the kittens sooner than that.

Nothing.

So maybe this would be completely easy. Maybe Chess wouldn't even come out when she rode by on the road. Maybe they wouldn't see each other until school started in September and they rode the high school bus together. It would be the four of them then, a school friendship, and that would be fine. Joni had plenty of friends she never saw except in school.

The house felt empty. Everybody else was making cheese or working outside. "Yeah, Mom, try to find someplace quiet!" Joni muttered.

She got out her 4-H binder and read the camp handouts. There was a timetable of stable inspections, a lesson schedule, and a long list of things she needed to have in her tack trunk. That's what she should do—clean Archie's tack. She'd have to do it every day while she was up there, but she should start with a good basic cleaning now. And that would impress Mrs. Abernathy!

It had been a long time since she'd soaped her saddle and hackamore. She got filthy, but it was fun to make the leather shine again. Mrs. Abernathy, though, would be looking for buckle gunk. Whatever that was.

Joni examined the hackamore buckles. They looked the way they always looked. She scraped at the dark-looking metal with her thumbnail.

It wasn't dark-looking metal. It was gunked-up, filthy metal!

She rubbed it with a cloth. That made a small difference. She went up to Dad's shop and got some steel wool out of the toolbox and polished the buckle with that until it glittered. *How many buckles were on this thing?*

She polished them all. When she was done, the leather surrounding the buckles was dull from flaked-off gunk. Joni soaped it again. Now the buckles had a light frosting of gray soap foam. At least this came off with a cloth, and, finally, the hackamore looked stellar. She couldn't wait for Mrs. Abernathy to see it.

Rosita's lunch was toasted cheese sandwiches with arugula and garlic chives, and iced tea brightened up with fresh bee balm. "Rosita used to make gourmet sandwiches with college cafeteria food!" Olivia said proudly. "She should totally have a restaurant someday."

"Or not," Rosita said. "It's about as good a way to go broke as farming!"

"Have a farm restaurant," Joni suggested. "Go broke twice as fast!"

Dad said, "So—I'm taking that baler part to get repaired this afternoon. Olivia and Tobin, you're milking, right? And I hope Rosita is cooking!"

"And I'm going to Mrs. Abernathy's for a riding lesson," Joni said.

"Thanks for letting me know. Let's help Rosita clean up."

"I'll do that," Joni said. It wasn't that she was in cleanup mode, exactly, but this day was lo-o-o-ng! Each hour seemed like a week. If she wasn't going to have a friend next door, she'd have to get herself up to Danae's and Alyssa's a lot more, in spite of the difficult ride.

Finally, it was time to head to her lesson. In honor of her polished tack, Joni put on a fancy riding shirt, the one she was planning to wear at camp on the final day. As she set out across the field, her heart pounded a little faster. Wave. Smile. Say hi and ride on. It had sounded easy this morning, but now she had to do it. At least it was true that she couldn't stop to talk. She had to get to Mrs. Abernathy's by three thirty . . .

Wave. Smile. "Hi!"

She rode down the trail. Along the gurgling brook. Out onto the road.

Across the bridge, the white house showed through the trees. Joni felt Archie hesitate. She turned her face straight at the house, feeling that align her whole body. Not her spirit, but she could fake that. "Walk on, Archie!"

He thudded across the bridge. The lawn was empty. The Venturas' car was parked beside the house, but there was no one in sight, and no one came out.

Was Chess watching out a window? Or was she upstairs in her bedroom with the celebrity posters, planning to free every animal in the world? Did she care that their friendship hadn't worked? Was she mad?

Passing the barn, Archie slowed, pointing his ears at the lush paddock. Joni looked through the open door, but no one was there, either. She felt disappointed, which surprised her. She'd been so relieved when Danae and Alyssa helped her figure out how not to be friends. But who would startle her anymore? Who would laugh like that, just about animals eating? Anyway, it wasn't Chess's fault that she didn't know things. She was smart. She could learn. She'd been pretty awful yesterday, but something bad had happened. Joni had never even found out what.

So it wasn't fair to judge her by that one visit. She was like

Archie, a challenge. And Joni might be a happy camper, but she was also "the kid who rides that gray pony." She wasn't someone who needed her life to be perfectly safe. Look at her now, heading off to a riding lesson with Mrs. Abernathy!

So she wasn't going to ride past, say hi, and be "friendly." She was going to be *friends* with Chess, if she could figure out—

Archie stiffened and stopped in his tracks. Then he whirled, staring across the Venturas' field. Joni saw someone running.

"Joni! *Help!*"

TWENTY

"I Can't Stop Them"

Chess came running toward Joni, stumbling in the long grass. Her breath came in loud gasps that Joni could hear halfway across the field. Archie raised his head in alarm and started to back away from her. Joni held him firm with her hands and legs, but fear flooded her stomach. Something terrible must have happened . . .

It seemed to take forever for Chess to get close—and too late, Joni realized she could have ridden to meet her. But Archie wouldn't have moved, and now Chess stood a few yards away, one hand pressed to her heaving chest.

"They're eating and I can't stop them!"

"Who?" Joni said. "Who's eating?"

"The ponies!" Chess pointed with her whole arm at the gap

between the trees that led to the back field. "Hurry!"

Cold suspicion trickled down Joni's spine. She goosed Archie in the ribs and trotted past Chess. He arched his neck as he went by her, and curved his body away, a kind of alarm he'd only ever showed the day he met his first llama. They went fast across the first field, toward the gap between the trees. As they neared it, Archie's neck came up again and his trot went hard and bouncy. He started a light snorting, like the rattle of a snare drum.

"It's okay," Joni said. "It's just your friends." She couldn't see anything but empty field.

Archie whinnied suddenly and rushed forward around the corner, and then Joni saw it. Tucked back against the woods was a sort of corral, small and rectangular, made of electric fence posts strung with strands and strands of baling twine.

"So *that's* it!"

Most of the twine looked tight and secure. Chess had worked hard on it, and it would have been a good fence if it were electric. The corral was partly in the woods, in an area where there wasn't much grass. So she had listened to Joni. She'd heard that much.

But there were no minis in the pen. A section of twine had been pushed up and down, and beyond it, JD stood with his nose plunged deep in lush clover, eating steadily. Kubota stood nearby, *not* eating.

Oh, good! Joni thought.

Oh, not good! Kubota buckled his knees and lowered himself to the ground.

For a moment, he just lay there. Then he raised his head

and looked at his own round side. He bit himself in the belly, flopped over, and started to roll.

"*No!*" Joni flung herself off Archie and reached for Kubota's head.

He had no halter on. There was nothing to grab.

Joni looked up. Way back near the gap, Chess was floundering through tall grass that wanted to tangle around her ankles and trip her.

"Where's his halter?" Joni screamed. "*Where* are their *halters?*"

Chess couldn't get a word out. She pointed behind Joni. Joni turned and there were the two small halters and lead ropes, neatly hung on a tree. On the ground underneath lay the tiny grazing muzzles.

Joni ran to the tree and grabbed the halters. When she turned, Kubota was up. Archie stood staring at him, too fascinated to either run away or start eating. Chess was close now, running much faster than it looked.

"Catch Archie!" Joni yelled. "Don't let—oh, no!"

Kubota went down again. Joni ran to him, but she had to wait for his hooves to stop waving in the air before she could get close to his head. She slipped the halter over his brown nose, buckled it firmly, and hauled on the lead rope with all her strength.

With a groan, Kubota propped himself up, sitting braced on his haunches like a dog. After a moment, he started to sag.

"*No!*" Joni leaned on the rope, and Kubota heaved to his feet.

He didn't shake himself, the way Archie did after a nice roll.

He just stood there with his small mouth pinched tight. His eyes looked dark and troubled, and his legs were quivery.

Joni towed him toward Archie and Chess, and pushed the rope into Chess's hand. "Walk him!"

Chess looked blank.

"You *have* to make him *walk!*" Joni said. "Don't let him lie—no!" She took the rope back and turned Kubota in a circle until he stiffened his quavering legs. "Don't let him lie down! Hit him if you have to!" Was she going to have to hit *Chess*? She was just standing there! "Do it!" Joni yelled. "If you let him roll, he could twist his intestines. He could *die!*"

At last, Chess took a step, tugging on the halter. Kubota didn't move.

"*Pull* him!" Joni went behind Kubota and pushed on his butt. He leaned back, resisting, and Chess pulled harder.

"He's so strong!"

"I *told* you they were strong!" Joni shoved again, Chess pulled, and Kubota unlocked his knees and took a reluctant step. Chess started him moving in a small circle, and Joni turned to look for Archie. He hadn't bolted, thank goodness! She grabbed his trailing reins.

Now what? Ride for help?

No, first she had to catch JD, before he ate himself sick, too.

She hurried toward the black mini, towing Archie behind her. JD lifted his head, looked at her for a moment, then trotted a few yards off and snatched another mouthful of clover.

Joni followed.

JD trotted away again.

"No, you don't, you little stinker!" Joni turned to Archie

and leaped for the saddle, grabbing the horn to pull herself up. Archie made a lunge, ready to gallop off home. Joni pulled him in a circle, all rein now, no finesse at all, and pointed him at JD, who looked alarmed and started trotting faster.

But Archie seemed to understand what Joni needed. He took off after the tiny black horse, passed him, and whirled to block him. Joni threw herself out of the saddle and wrapped her arms and the rope around JD's neck.

JD surged against her for a second, striking her shin with one hard hoof and almost breaking free. Then he surrendered, relaxing. Joni pulled the halter on, Archie poking his nose curiously over her shoulder. She pushed the two animals apart and led them both over to Chess. Kubota's legs were trying to buckle again.

"Keep him moving!" Joni ordered. She tied JD to a tree, making sure the knot was horse-proof, and turned around. "I have to go get help. You don't have your phone, right?"

Chess shook her head. She didn't look panicked anymore. She was towing Kubota strongly, with a determined look. "Can't *you* help him? You know all about horses—"

"No," Joni said. "A horse with colic needs a vet. He could die! Or he could founder—"

"Then *she* won't be able to drive him!" Chess snapped.

"Then he won't be able to *walk*!" Joni said. "Don't you know what happens to them? All the sensitive part inside their hooves swells up, but it can't go anywhere because it's inside the hard part. Their *bones* get pushed out of shape! They'll do anything not to put weight on their own front feet!" She felt tears hot on her cheeks, and brushed them away with the back of her hand.

Chess stopped walking Kubota, staring at Joni with a horrified look on her face. This time, finally, Joni had gotten through. What if she'd tried harder before? Maybe she could have prevented all this.

But there was no time for that now. "Is your mom ho—"

No. Chess's mother must be home because the car was there. But she would be flustered, she'd need explanations. Joni knew for sure that Mrs. Abernathy was home. She would know exactly which vet to call. Kubota should have a vet who knew him, and right away.

She pulled herself into the saddle and wheeled Archie around, groping for her right stirrup. Chess looked like she wanted to fall to the ground and curl up like a caterpillar. So, good, she was sorry! That wouldn't help Kubota. "Walk him!" Joni said.

Chess started, and took a firmer hold on the rope. "I'm sorry, but you have to walk." Her face was bleached white, her voice determined. When Kubota didn't move, she whirled the end of the lead rope and popped him on the butt. He took a few steps, and then a few more. She was going to keep him going. Joni released the reins.

Archie shot across the field. Joni didn't think she'd ever ridden so fast, not even that day at camp when he ran away with her. Would they make the turn at the gap in the trees?

She aimed her face that way, fiercely, and Archie swooped around the turn. In spite of everything being so terribly wrong, Joni let out a whoop as she felt his muscles bunch. "I love you, Archie!"

They came to the road, and Joni prepared to haul him around

in the opposite direction than he would want to go. But when she set her face toward Mrs. Abernathy's, Archie turned easily. His hooves rattled on the hard gravel as he sprinted straight down North Valley Road, his silver mane flying in Joni's eyes.

She pulled him up at Mrs. Abernathy's mailbox and turned him down the driveway. Mrs. Abernathy stood out by the shed. The electric fence gate was open. The two plastic gate handles lay on the ground. Mrs. Abernathy was looking out across the unfenced part of the field. The grass was trampled there, where Chess must have led the minis.

Mrs. Abernathy turned to Joni, her face fierce. "They've been stolen."

"Yes," Joni said. "My friend took them."

Mrs. Abernathy's cheeks reddened. Her eyes flared with an icy light. "JD's okay," Joni said, her voice wobbling now, "but Kubota's got colic. He's trying to roll. Chess is walking him and—"

"Where?" Mrs. Abernathy took out her phone.

"The white house—" Joni pointed. "Way out in the back field, behind the barn—"

Mrs. Abernathy punched in a phone number. "Sue?" she said after a moment. "One of my minis has colic. Yes, it's an emergency—I see. Have him call this number when he can. The animal isn't at my place, and I'm not sure just where I'll be." She took the phone from her ear, giving it a vicious tweak with her thumb. "Perfect! He's out on a farm call, at least an hour away." She took a swift step toward her car and doubled over, pressing one hand to her hip.

"Give me your phone," Joni said. "I'll call Dad."

Mrs. Abernathy handed Joni the phone without speaking. Her face was rigid, her eyes bright and angry. She slid stiffly behind the wheel of her car, backed around, and took off in a spurt of gravel.

Joni let Archie graze beside the driveway while she struggled with the unfamiliar phone. As it finally rang, she realized Dad wasn't going to answer. He wasn't home. He was off getting a part fixed—

"Hello?" It was Rosita.

"Is Olivia there?" Joni asked.

"Is this Joni? They're milking. Can I help?"

"No, I need—" She needed Dad and the truck. But Dad had taken the truck. "There's a sick horse," she said. "We need— could I just talk to Olivia?"

"Is it your horse? Are you okay?"

"Not Archie. One of Mrs. Abernathy's." Joni was riding back up the driveway as she talked, the phone pressed to her ear, trying to guide and slow Archie with one hand on the reins. "He's at Chess's house, way in a back field—"

"I'll get them," Rosita said. "Meet us by the road."

Suddenly, Joni heard the compressor motor over the phone. A sheep bleated. Rosita had gone outside. She must be close to the barn now.

"But they're milking—"

"They'll stop milking," Rosita said. "Hang in there, Joni. We're on our way."

TWENTY-ONE

"You Girls"

Joni fumbled the phone into the pocket of her shirt. She galloped back to the Venturas' barn. Mrs. Abernathy's car was parked there, and she was way out in the field, almost to the gap, limping, but moving fast.

What would she say to Chess? It was going to be terrible. Joni was glad she had to wait out here. Music drifted out the window of the white house. Mrs. Ventura had no idea . . . But where was Olivia? Come *on*!

Finally, she heard an engine sound. In a moment, Tobin's van came wheezing around the corner, so fast it looked like all four wheels were off the ground. Joni could see three people inside it—so Rosita had come, too. The van angled into the barn driveway and Olivia jumped out.

"Joni, are you okay?"

"Yes, but Chess stole Mrs. Abernathy's minis!" Joni pointed out across the field, along the trail of trampled grass. "One of them has colic. I rode to Mrs. Abernathy's and she called the vet, but he can't come and Kubota's rolling. Olivia, I think it's really bad!"

Olivia pushed her hand up into her hair, like she was trying to squeeze her thoughts back into her skull. "Did you have *any* idea she was going to do this?"

Joni shook her head. She should have. It seemed obvious now. "But, Olivia, if the vet can't come—"

"Right," Olivia said. "Pony first. Tobin, can we—?" She pointed out across the field.

Tobin shrugged. "Should be able to. Hop in!"

Olivia slammed the door, and he drove straight toward the edge of the driveway. The van dipped, with a slight crunching sound, then rolled smoothly across the field, grass swishing against the back bumper. Archie surged past it, in a hurry to get to his new friends.

In the back field, Mrs. Abernathy was towing Kubota toward the gap. But she couldn't walk fast enough to keep him moving. He buckled his knees and lay down again, stretching his neck against the pull of the rope. Chess just stood there, her face white and shiny with tears and her hands twisted into the hem of her shirt. By the corral, JD tugged at the tree he was tied to, sending shrill whinnies after his friend. Archie answered. Chess looked up with a start.

She stared at Joni. Then she ran toward the woods and came racing back with a branch in her hand. She brought it down on Kubota's rump. Once. Twice.

Kubota propped himself up again and lurched to his feet. He braced against Mrs. Abernathy and she winced, pressing her hand to her hip.

Chess reached for the lead rope. "I'll lead him. He was moving for me!"

Mrs. Abernathy's expression was worse than any words. She turned away from Chess and hobbled another step. Kubota stretched his neck and braced his legs. The van pulled up, Olivia and Rosita hopping out as Chess pushed on Kubota's butt. "I'm sorry! I'm so sorry—"

"*Sorry?*" Mrs. Abernathy turned with a fierce laugh. "That won't save his life, will it, you stupid girl! Horses don't need people who understand their feelings. They need people who understand what they *are*, and how to keep them from killing themselves!"

Chess turned even paler. Her dark eyes were huge. She looked helpless and very small. Olivia said gently, "She's only a kid."

"That *kid* just killed my horse!"

Joni felt that like a punch in the stomach. But Tobin said, "She hasn't killed him yet." He slid open the side door of the van. "Olivia, Joni, where do we take him?"

Take him! Of course! Kubota would fit in the van, just as well as he would in Dad's truck. He didn't need to wait for a vet to come to him. "Countryside," Joni said. "The clinic down on the highway. They're the best."

"Somebody call them," Tobin said. "Tell them we're coming."

"As if I could afford them!" Mrs. Abernathy said bitterly.

Tobin looked startled. After a moment, he asked, "*Can* you?"

Mrs. Abernathy raised a hand to her mouth. Joni saw it tremble. "Yes, yes!" she said. "Go ahead! It's only money!"

Rosita whipped out her phone. "Wow, I've got a signal! Okay." Her thumbs danced. She shook her hair back and put the phone to her ear, stepping away from the group.

Tobin climbed into the van and dragged the mattress off his bed. He wedged it in front of the cook stove and put a milk crate full of books out of the way between the front seats. Then he jumped out.

"Ready?"

Together, he and Olivia maneuvered Kubota to the door. Hands linked behind his haunches, they half-lifted, half-pushed him into the van, and he collapsed onto Tobin's mattress.

Tobin turned to Mrs. Abernathy. "Do you want to ride with us, ma'am, or follow in your car?"

"With you," Mrs. Abernathy said. "Somebody should sit on him, keep him from rolling."

Chess said, "I'll do that. Please? Let me help?"

Mrs. Abernathy flushed red and pressed her lips firmly together, turning to Joni. "Get JD home," she said. "Lock him in the barn. After that—" She gave an undignified gulp, like she was trying to catch her breath. "After that, I never want to see you girls on my place again!"

TWENTY-TWO

Brave

For a second, Joni didn't understand. Everyone else stopped moving, stopped speaking. Shocked faces turned toward Mrs. Abernathy.

"*Joni* didn't—" Chess started.

Kubota lay on his side, clunking his head against something. Olivia glanced at him. Red triangles flared on her cheeks, something that only happened when she was very angry.

"Rosita, hop in and sit on him," she said in a quiet voice. "You guys go. I'm staying here with my sister."

She turned to Mrs. Abernathy. "Are your keys in your car, ma'am?" She made the word *ma'am* sound like an insult. "We left sixty sheep waiting to be milked, and I need to get back to them."

Mrs. Abernathy felt in her pocket and came up empty. "They must be in it." She turned away, pulling herself into the passenger seat of the van. Rosita lay across Kubota's body. Tobin closed the side door. A moment later, the van rolled away.

Olivia looked up at Joni. "That. Old. *Bat!* You okay, Joni?"

Joni didn't know. Her face felt numb and everything seemed far away, everything except the memory of Mrs. Abernathy's blazing blue eyes. And why was Mrs. Abernathy mad at *her*?

Olivia reached up and gripped her hand. "You did not deserve that, Joni!" She paused and took a breath. "No. We need to cut her some slack. She's very worried—"

Chess gave a dry, shaky sob. "Will he *die*?"

Olivia squeezed Joni's hand again and turned to Chess. "Probably not. Don't you think, Joni? I mean, horses *can* die from colic, but most of the time, they don't."

But ponies were different than horses—tougher in some ways, more delicate in others. Joni didn't know about minis.

"It happened so *fast*!" Chess said. "I did listen to you, Joni! I tried! But I thought they'd stay in their fence, and then I couldn't catch them, and—I only *had* them a couple of hours!"

There was nothing to say. Things could go really bad, really quickly, with animals. People, too.

"Well, let's get the other guy home," Olivia said. "I left the sheep standing in their stanchions. When Daddy gets back, he's going to think we were abducted by aliens!"

"Are the sheep *okay*?" Chess asked in a quavering voice.

"Oh!" Olivia waved her hand dismissively. "They're fine! They're just standing there bleating and pooping."

She untied Joni's complicated knot. JD put his head down

to eat, but Olivia pulled it up and marched him across the field. Chess walked beside him, one hand on his back the whole way.

Archie followed. Joni didn't guide him. She just let him carry her. She felt so strange, like time had slowed down, and it might take them the rest of their lives to cross this field.

When they reached the road, Mrs. Ventura stood in the doorway of the white house. She wore a big shirt over her regular clothes, flecked and spattered with yellow paint. She watched them come but kept glancing behind her, probably at Noah.

"Francesca?" she called, when they were close enough. "What's going on? Isn't that one of the ponies from down the road?"

Chess nodded.

Mrs. Ventura looked from her to Olivia, then to Joni, and back to Chess. "Oh, no," she said. "You *didn't*!"

"She did," Olivia said. "Sorry. The other pony is sick. My friends took it to the vet."

Mrs. Ventura closed her eyes. "Oh, Chess. Did your grand— no. We'll talk about that later. How sick is the pony?" she asked Olivia. "What can we do to help?"

"He's pretty sick," Olivia said.

"Where's the vet's office? I'll call my husband and have him meet the owner there. Is this one okay?" she asked, frowning at JD.

"So far! Why don't you girls take him down the road," Olivia told Joni and Chess. "I'll come along with the car in a minute." She pushed the lead rope into Chess's reluctant hand. Mrs. Ventura started to say something and stopped herself.

Wearily, Joni turned Archie around. She felt like she'd been riding up and down North Valley Road for hours. Archie was happy to be with his new friend, but he walked much faster than JD. When he got too far ahead, JD whinnied, and Joni stopped to wait. She didn't look back, but she could hear Chess crying.

She felt like crying, too. Mrs. Abernathy was mean and unfair, and Joni shouldn't even care. Because what did it matter what a mean person thought—a loud, surprising sob burst out of her.

"Oh, *Joni*!"

Chess sounded so sorry that Joni couldn't stop the tears. She fell forward onto Archie's neck. "I *hate* her!"

A hand closed around her clenched fist. "I'm sorry," Chess said. "I wish I'd listened to you."

"I wish I'd *made* you listen!"

"Nobody can," Chess said. "That's the problem."

Archie jerked under Joni, and she heard a tiny squeal. She looked up as the two horses touched noses. JD squealed again and struck out with his front foot.

Joni straightened in the saddle, sniffing loudly. "Don't let him do that," she said, and Chess pulled JD away. Joni looked down on her bent dark head.

She had made Chess listen. Not soon enough. Not closely enough. But Chess *had* listened to her, at least somewhat. If Joni had tried harder, maybe none of this would have happened. It was her mistake, too, a little bit, and if Kubota died, it would be a little bit her fault.

Be okay! she thought at him, way down there at Countryside Clinic. *Be okay!*

They turned up Mrs. Abernathy's drive, past the potato field and the big garden. Joni remembered the three of them out there, Mrs. Abernathy so big and powerful, and the little team so well behaved. The potato plants looked glossy green, the garden was neat, and beside the barn was a pile of small logs, ready to be cut up for firewood. The minis had helped do all that.

Joni got off and handed Chess Archie's reins. She led JD past the cart and the tiny harnesses hanging on the wall and shut him in his barn. Chess stood leaning against Archie, looking scared and exhausted.

"What were you going to *do* with them?" Joni asked. Chess was smart. She must have had a plan.

Chess gulped. "It would have worked. If I was right. I mean—I knew she'd find them and the police would come, but so would the TV cameras, and it would all come out in public, and they'd be saved." She sniffed, and said in a quieter voice, "And Nana would hear about it."

"Oh," Joni said. There weren't so many TV cameras here. This wasn't California. But more was going on than just the animals. It was about Chess's grandmother. Some of it—

"And I wanted to be like you," Chess said.

"Like *me*?" Joni said.

Chess nodded. "I mean—you wouldn't do what I did, because you knew they didn't need rescuing. But you're brave! You ride all by yourself, you go anywhere you want—you *do* stuff! Real stuff! And I need to be like that, because it's just me now—"

"I'm the biggest coward there is!" Joni said. She'd hardly dared to ride past Chess's house just an hour or two ago.

"No," Chess said. "You're amazing. If these horses *were* in trouble, you'd just rescue them."

"No, I'd tell Kalysta," Joni said. She was absolutely clear on that.

Mrs. Abernathy's car pulled in. Olivia got out and checked that JD's gate was shut. "I totally trust you, Joni, but I don't want—I don't want her saying you didn't do everything perfectly." She paused, watching JD. "He looks okay, doesn't he?"

JD was wandering around the barn picking up stray wisps of hay. He kept lifting his head to listen, probably wondering where Kubota was. "He'll be back soon," Joni wanted to tell him, but she couldn't force the words out. They might not be true.

"Hop in, Chess," Olivia said. "I'll drop you back home. You okay by yourself, Joni?"

Not really. Joni wanted to be the one getting into the car. She wanted somebody to take care of her. But she and Archie had to get each other home. She nodded. Olivia looked hard at her for a moment, with a worried frown swirling her eyebrows together.

"Be safe," she said. "I'll see you at the farm in a few minutes." She drove away, and Joni rode slowly after her. Shrill whinnies from JD followed them down the road. When Joni passed Chess's house, Mrs. Abernathy's car was still parked at the bottom of the driveway. Chess and Olivia sat in it, talking.

What would happen to Chess? Would she have to go to court? Because what she did was stealing. It was even abuse.

But she tried. She did the best she could, with the little bit she knew. If Chess had to go to court, Joni would have to go, too, and stand up and say that.

And what if Kubota died? It wouldn't be murder. He was an animal, and Chess didn't mean to do it. But she would have killed him. *Don't die!* Joni thought.

Halfway across the big field, she saw Mrs. Abernathy's car sweep into the farmyard. So, good, Olivia was back. But Joni couldn't just go to the milking parlor. She had to take care of Archie first, give him a rubdown and some carrots. Archie was the hero, and he'd worked very hard. He must have been tired, because he let Joni hug his neck for a long minute before he got bored and walked away.

Joni went into the milking parlor. Dad was back, milking sheep and listening to Olivia with a wide-eyed, amazed expression. "Joni!" he said when he saw her, and opened his arms.

The hug made Joni cry again. Dad patted her back and rested his chin on her head, and she hid in the dark space next to his chest until she absolutely had to blow her nose. Olivia handed her a piece of paper towel.

"Mom's on her way home," Dad said.

"You didn't need to call her."

"Yeah, I did. She'd be really upset if I didn't. You hungry? Want something to eat?"

Joni shook her head. "I'll just help you guys milk."

Not that there was anything for her to do, but this was a good place to be. The swish of the milking machines drowned out other sounds. The clean smells of wet concrete, disinfectant, and milk, the gray-white sheep on their metal platform, under the whitewashed ceiling—it all made a small, safe world, and Joni wanted to stay right here.

They were milking the last batch of sheep when the Bears began to bark. Joni braced herself. Mom would have so many questions. She'd have to tell the whole story . . .

But the person who walked through the door was Tobin, and behind him came Mrs. Abernathy.

TWENTY-THREE

"One of Us"

Mrs. Abernathy came straight to Joni, looking her directly in the eyes. "Will you accept my apology? I was angry and frightened, and I took it out on the wrong person."

"That's okay," Joni said stiffly.

Mrs. Abernathy tipped her head slightly to one side, like she was replaying Joni's words, listening very carefully. With a quick, sad smile, she said, "No, it's not. I'm sorry. I need to get my phone from you, Joni, and then I'll take myself out of your way."

Joni had forgotten the phone. She looked down at her pocket and saw that her good shirt was dirty from tackling JD. The corner of the pocket was ripped. The phone was still there, though. She held it out to Mrs. Abernathy. *Take it,* she thought. *Go away.*

But when their fingers brushed, Joni felt a tremor in Mrs. Abernathy's hand. Startled, she looked up. Mrs. Abernathy's face was white and exhausted. Her eyes stared off at something that wasn't here. She looked like Chess, like Kubota.

"How is he doing?" Joni asked.

Mrs. Abernathy's face relaxed a little. "When I left, he was nibbling hay."

"Great," Joni said. It was an excellent sign when an animal started to eat again.

"The little beasts aren't very stoic," Mrs. Abernathy said. "He perked right up after a dose of painkillers. I'm actually more worried about JD. I imagine he just kept pigging out. Was it you who tied him up?"

Joni nodded.

"Thank you," Mrs. Abernathy said. "That was exactly the right thing to do." She hesitated. "I'm ashamed to have lumped you girls together. It was stupid and unwarranted—as Rosita and Tobin pointed out to me—and I hope you'll forgive me. I've enjoyed your friendship, Joni." She sounded humble and respectful, and that made Joni feel grown up, like someone who could have an adult friend. Who *did* have an adult friend.

"Me, too," she said. "I mean—yes."

Mrs. Abernathy's face softened. "Thank you. I appreciate that."

She held out her hand, and Joni shook it awkwardly. She wasn't used to shaking hands. Something more needed to be said now, didn't it? Something about Chess?

But Mrs. Abernathy was already turning away. "I need to get some medicine into JD."

"Do you need help?" Dad asked.

Mrs. Abernathy shook her head. "No, thank you. The day I can't take care of them myself is the day I find them a new home. I will need my car keys, though."

"They're in it," Olivia said, not turning from the sheep.

"Thank you," Mrs. Abernathy said. "Thanks to all of you."

Nobody said anything until they heard the car door slam. Then Olivia turned around. "Wow, Joni! You are so much nicer than I am!"

"Joni is a gentle soul," Dad said, wrapping one arm around her shoulders.

"Actually, she's very strong," Rosita said. "Maybe you mean that kind of gentle?"

"And brave," Tobin said.

"And smart and responsible," Rosita said. "We pointed that out to Mrs. Abernathy. She was apologizing before we got to the end of North Valley Road!"

Joni felt her cheeks burn. She turned her face into Dad's sleeve.

"She's one tough old lady," Tobin said. "She wouldn't even talk to that kid's father!"

Dad said, "I can understand that! If somebody stole one of my animals and injured it, I'd find it hard to be forgiving."

Tobin said, "He told the vet to send him the bills."

"Good. Ruth doesn't have much money to spend."

It's only money! Joni remembered her saying. So that was irony or something. The potato field and firewood weren't hobbies. Mrs. Abernathy needed them, and she needed her minis to help do the work. She loved them, too, obviously, but

160

that was nobody's business as long as she took good care of them.

"I need to call Chess," she said.

Dad looked down at her, eyebrows raised.

"I want to tell her that Kubota was eating," Joni said.

"So—friends again?" Dad said. "Even after all this?"

"She's not a bad kid," Olivia said. Joni was startled. "We talked in the car for a while. Call her, Joni. She was pretty devastated."

Joni did call when they all went back to the house. All she got was a robot lady's voice, inviting her to leave a message.

Rosita's supper plans had been completely upended. When Mom walked in, she was making toasted cheese sandwiches again. Mom sat down at the table, and everyone told her the story at once. The voices came from all sides, and soon there were more. Somehow the news had gotten out. Willow called, and then Li Min, and then Grandma DeeDee, all wanting to hear the story. So did Kate, from way down in South Carolina. When she'd gotten the whole thing from Olivia, she wanted to talk to Joni.

"Hey," she said. "I just told Olivia—today's the day you turned into one of the Big Girls. You're not just this cute little kid anymore. You're one of us."

"Oh," Joni said. "Wow." Coming from Kate, that was huge. "Thank you."

"Don't thank me!" Kate said. "Thank yourself. You're the one who did it."

Joni hung up, feeling a glow in her chest—but also starting to feel like she did at the end of a long school day, hungry for peace and quiet. She slipped away from the table and went out to check on Archie. He seemed perky and bright-eyed, ready for more. Joni got him a carrot. As she stood it on end in her hand, she remembered that first day when Chess fed him a carrot and laughed, and they became friends. What was happening to Chess? After the dog crate incident, her parents moved all the way across the country. How could they top that? Boarding school? The moon?

The day replayed in her head like a video—an indie docudrama with a shaky handheld camera. She kept seeing Chess's wet, white face, and her insanely well-made, completely useless baling twine fence. Then the tiny work harnesses hanging so neatly on Mrs. Abernathy's shed wall popped into her head. Mrs. Abernathy's shed and barn were so carefully set up, so precisely maintained—

Like Chess's fence.

What if Chess actually *knew* anything? She'd be a horsewoman just like Mrs. Abernathy—everything correct and by the book. They really should be friends—

But that would never happen. Even if Chess didn't get sent to boarding school, she and Mrs. Abernathy could never, ever be friends. The most Joni could hope for was that everybody would be okay.

Archie pricked his ears toward the stall door, and in a moment, Mom appeared. "Hello, you two." She came in and gave Archie a neck scratch in the place he loved most. "What a day, huh? I wanted to check if you're okay. Your dad and Olivia said you were pretty upset earlier."

Joni said, "I just wish people would answer their phone!"

"Don't be surprised if you don't hear from Chess for a while," Mom said. "That family has a lot on its plate."

"I should have stopped her," Joni said.

"Did you know what she was going to do?"

"No. But I knew she thought they were abused, and I kept not—it just seemed like she was never going to listen to me, so I stopped trying. But she *did* listen. She tried to keep them from eating too much. So if I'd tried harder—"

"Like how?" Mom asked. "What could you have said?"

Good question! "Like—don't steal people's horses? I don't know."

"If you think you could have tried harder, I believe you," Mom said. "But probably you couldn't have prevented this. Chess is a very strong-minded girl. People like that need to make big mistakes in order to learn, and even that doesn't always work."

"Am *I* strong-minded?" Joni asked.

Mom considered. "You know, you are," she said after a moment. "You're stable. You don't let other people knock you off balance. That's a different kind of strength, and it's easy to miss because you're quiet, but Chess is helping you with that. If you stay friends, I think you'll make quite a pair!"

Joni liked the sound of that. "We're friends," she said. Well, she could say that. *She* was a friend.

In her room later, she was nearly asleep, covered in kittens, when the door opened. "It's me," Olivia said softly. "Can I get in with you?"

That was what Joni used to say when she was little and

couldn't sleep, and she went into Kate's or Olivia's room. In a moment, she felt Olivia's warm body behind her and Olivia's arm around her, Olivia's breath in her hair. They were quiet. The mother cat hopped onto the bed and nestled on top of them.

"What did you talk about with Chess?" Joni asked after a few minutes. "In the car."

"Her grandmother," Olivia said. "That is one sad little kid, whatever else she is. I mean, think about it, Joni! Even before her brother was born, their parents were completely focused on him. The grandmother *raised* Chess—and now they're separated, totally. That's half the reason they moved here, to get Chess away from her."

"Well," Joni said. "I mean—a *dog crate*?"

"I know," Olivia said. "It must have been upsetting for them, what happened at the circus. But can you do that to a kid? Move her all the way across the country to keep her away from the person she loves most?"

"I hope she's okay," Joni said.

"Me, too," Olivia said. "You are, right?"

She hugged Joni a little tighter. And that was the last thing Joni knew, until a kitten started licking her ear a little after sunrise.

TWENTY-FOUR

On the Bridge

Mrs. Abernathy called while Joni was eating breakfast to say that Kubota and JD were both okay, and Kubota was coming home that morning. "And, Joni, I won't embarrass you by thanking you over and over. But just this one more time—thank you! I still owe you a riding lesson. When is camp?"

"It starts on Saturday."

"That won't work. A lesson afterward, then, to consolidate what you've learned? Just remember—look where you want the horse to go. That's half the battle!"

After she hung up, Joni dialed the Venturas' number. She got the robotic lady again. "Hi, this is Joni," she said after the beep. "The minis are both okay, so . . ." So what? How should she finish that sentence? "So call me."

And the phone did ring, but it was Danae, asking if she and Alyssa could come hear the story. "Sure," Joni said.

But how was she going to tell it? It would be easy if she weren't planning to be friends with Chess. Then she could just shock them, and they could all look down on Chess and talk about how stupid and irresponsible she had been. Now Joni wanted to make them *like* Chess.

As soon as they were all in her room, she said, "I'm friends with her again. I think."

"Wait, really?" Alyssa said.

"I don't care. I'm not letting her near Pumpkin!" Danae said.

"What if she steals Archie?" Alyssa asked. "What if she steals your dad's sheep? They do that, these animal rights people. They, like, open chicken houses and break fences, and let animals out."

"She won't," Joni said. "She knows she made a big mistake."

"So what *happened*?" Alyssa asked.

Joni told them, skipping Mrs. Abernathy's anger and Chess's crying. She focused on Tobin's van charging to the rescue, and on Archie. "And I bulldogged JD," she said. "Just like a rodeo cowboy bulldogging a steer. I just *tackled* him." It was pretty cool, actually. She would never have dreamed she knew how to do that.

After they'd heard the story twice, Danae asked, "Have you started packing?"

Joni hadn't, so they got out the camp checklist and went to work. When it came to "Neat, short-sleeved shirt for showing," Joni held up the shirt she'd worn yesterday.

"Nope," Alyssa said. "Time to go shopping."

After lunch, Mom took them to town, where Alyssa, a genius shopper, found Joni a great shirt at the secondhand store for five dollars. Then, they went to the food cart for maple ice cream.

Ice cream. A dairy product. Chess wouldn't eat it, but Joni wished she were there. She could eat sorbet, anyway.

On the way home, Mom turned down North Valley Road. It was a bit of a detour. "I thought you might be able to tell if she's gotten the pony back."

"Thanks," Joni said. She leaned forward, trying to see around the corners and through the trees.

Several birds flew up from the ground as they neared Mrs. Abernathy's mailbox. "What are they eating?" Alyssa asked. "Is that *cake*? It looks like cake!"

Mom slowed the car down. Joni looked for the minis. Of course, they were nowhere in sight. The car swept toward Chess's house. Mom slowed there, too, but no one was outdoors.

Joni slumped back against the seat, and Mom reached over to squeeze her knee. Then she put both hands on the wheel to make the sharp corner.

"Joni, look!" Danae pointed toward the bridge.

Someone stood at the rail, gazing into the brook. No, it was two people, side by side with their arms around each other. The taller one, a woman, rested her cheek on top of the other person's head.

The second person was Chess.

"Oh!" Joni said. "It's her grandmother!"

"She got here fast!" Mom said.

Joni twisted in her seat to watch them as long as possible, but Chess and her grandmother didn't move. They just stayed deep in that long, warm hug.

TWENTY-FIVE

Equals

That evening, when Joni called, Chess's mother answered. "Oh, hello, Joni. I'll see if Francesca can come to the phone."

Joni knew what that meant—*see if she wants to talk to you.* She heard an unfamiliar voice in the background, and suddenly Chess was there in her ear, saying hi. Her voice sounded small and tentative.

"Hi," Joni said. "They're okay. Mrs. Abernathy called this morning. And Kubota's home."

"I know," Chess said. "The vet called Dad."

Joni listened to the silence. What should she say next? "Goodbye" would be easiest, and it was what she wanted to say, now that she'd actually gotten Chess on the phone. But that was stupid!

"So, your grandmother came," she said. "I saw you guys on the bridge."

"Yes," Chess said. "Joni—"

"Sorry," Joni said. "This probably isn't a good time."

"No, it's just . . ."

"I'm going to riding camp in two days," Joni said. "For a whole week. So, do you want to come see the kittens tomorrow? They're growing really fast."

Chess hesitated. "Would that be okay?"

"Yes!" Joni said. "Of course!" She sounded dramatic to herself, like Alyssa.

"I meant, with your parents," Chess said. "I stole somebody's animals, Joni. Why would they want me around?" She sounded older, tired.

"Do you *want* to come?" Joni asked.

"I'll call you back," Chess said abruptly, and hung up.

Was that good? Or not good? Whichever, it didn't happen soon. After waiting awhile, Joni wandered out to the picnic table where they all seemed to live this summer. Dad, Olivia, and Tobin were planning tomorrow's haying and milking. Rosita was telling Mom about her goal of studying at the CIA— the Culinary Institute of America, not the spy agency. "So if you want to not cook this summer," she said, "it would be great practice for me. You could go back to your writing retreat—"

"Or I could do my retreat right here on the farm," Mom said, reaching out to hug Joni.

The phone rang. Joni answered, but it wasn't Chess. A man asked to speak to Dad, who put his eyebrows way up and took the phone out of earshot for a long time. When he came back, he still looked surprised, and thoughtful.

"Who was it?" Mom asked.

"Chess's father," Dad said. "He wanted to be sure we're comfortable having Chess here, after what happened."

"What did you say?" Joni asked.

"I said, 'Sure.'" Dad sounded like he wanted to leave it at that.

"Daddy!" Olivia said. "That's so not *all* he said!"

"No," Dad agreed. "I respect him. They're a family with some things to work out, but he loves his daughter, and he loves his mother-in-law. She got on a plane the minute she heard about this. Got here at two in the morning, with only a toothbrush in her back pocket!"

"Are you comfortable having *her* on the farm?" Mom asked.

"That's not a question I was asked," Dad said.

"But—is Chess coming?" Joni asked.

Dad said, "I'm not sure. Her grandmother is only here for one more day. Chess doesn't want to miss any time with her. And I gather her self-confidence has taken a knock. It's not just about us feeling comfortable. It's also about her."

"Oh, poor kid!" Mom said. "Give her a little time, Joni. I'm sure she'll work it out."

But there wasn't time. Joni would be gone for a week, and Chess might lose even more self-confidence. It was like falling off a horse. You had to get right back on, or your fears grew.

Chess didn't call all day Thursday or all Friday morning. Joni was busy doing laundry and packing. She would have two lives next week—seven thirty to four at riding camp, and the rest of the time at a nearby campground with the 4-H group.

She needed riding things, stable things, camping things, and swimming things, warm clothes and rain clothes, and everything else for a week away from home.   ·

And she needed to play with the kittens because a week was a long time in a kitten's life. She needed to hang out in the milking parlor with Olivia and Tobin, and help Rosita on the hay wagon, and get extra hugs from Mom and Dad. A week was a long time in her life, too.

Still, Friday was also long. Danae and Alyssa had helped her pack the tack trunk, so Archie's things were ready. By the afternoon, Joni was, too. She kept looking down across the big field, hoping to see someone coming.

Maybe she should ride to North Valley Road. Maybe Chess would be outside, or maybe Joni would just ride up to the door and ask for her. But she didn't want to get Archie's tack dirty. She'd cleaned his bridle again this morning, paying special attention to buckle gunk.

So putting that bridle back on Archie wasn't going to happen. But as Joni wandered into the barn for the umpteenth time, she noticed a ratty old spare halter on its peg. On the floor was a heap of baling twine. *Hmm.*

She put on her riding helmet, haltered Archie, and tied baling twine into the side rings. She'd ridden him in a halter before. It hadn't gone well, but this time, she was optimistic. She led him to the big rock and slid onto his bare back.

Archie barged off. The twine dug into Joni's hands. After a few steps, he shoved his head down and started to eat.

Okay, this was a less-than-stellar idea! Joni kicked Archie into motion, circling him as she shortened the reins. *Look where you want the horse to go.* She turned her head toward the barn. In a moment, Archie turned that way, too. *Thank you, Mrs. Abernathy!* Joni settled into the curve of his back. Now she could use her legs softly to ask him to move. Light tugs on the baling twine kept him from trotting. With every step, she felt less like she was going to fall off, more like she was part of him.

She rode around back to where Dad was stacking bales. "I'm riding to Chess's house," she called.

"Okay," he called back. He couldn't see the halter and baling twine arrangement, which was probably just as well. She rode down the field and entered the woods, where Archie came to a sudden halt.

Joni clutched his mane with both hands to keep from falling. A dark-haired girl was walking her bike away from them down the brook trail. Archie snorted. The girl turned her head.

"Chess!"

"Hi," Chess said. "I was coming—"

"You were *going!*"

Chess didn't smile. "I chickened out." She turned her bike and wheeled it toward them.

"Well, come on," Joni said. "We'll go together."

Chess frowned. "I don't know—"

"The kittens need to see different people," Joni said. "So they don't get shy."

That wasn't exactly true. Once kittens got the idea that people were a source of food and entertainment, they liked everybody. It was puppies that got shy with strangers. But Chess didn't seem to know that. After a moment, she leaned her bike against a tree and followed Archie back into the field. Joni slid off so they could walk together.

It was hard to think what to say, though. Actually, it was impossible. They just walked until Chess suddenly asked, "Have you seen her?"

"Mrs. Abernathy? No," Joni said. "Not since—no."

"I made her a cake," Chess said.

"Oh, no!" Joni said. "I saw that. By the mailbox."

"I get it," Chess said. "I'd never forgive anybody who kidnapped Noah! But you could tell her—I'm not doing rescue anymore. I almost killed a horse. I don't want to make another huge mistake."

She didn't sound un-self-confident. She sounded very sure of herself, just in a negative way. "Some animals need to be rescued," Joni said, thinking of Patrick.

"But how would I *know*?" Chess asked. "I thought I knew before, but I was wrong!"

"Well—ask me!" Joni said. "And you could join 4-H. Come work at Kalysta's. Mrs. Abernathy helps there, too. She's on the Angels list."

Chess looked down at the grass under her feet. "I was wrong. About everything."

"No," Joni said. "I mean—*those* horses were fine, but lots of horses aren't. Like, there's this horse at Kalysta's that was locked in his stall and starved. If you lived next door to him, you wouldn't have gone, 'Oh, I guess she's sold him.' You would have found out, a lot sooner than his neighbors did!" The moment she said that, she knew it was true. The binoculars and notebook would have come into play, and Patrick would have been out of there before his neck bones started to show.

After a moment, Chess nodded. "Yes. I guess I would."

"You totally would! So come to Kalysta's. You'll learn a lot. We even ride the horses sometimes. It helps them get adopted, if Kalysta can say that a kid can ride them."

"I don't know how to ride."

"You could learn," Joni said. "Want to get on Archie right now?"

Of course, Chess wouldn't—would she? She stared at Archie, eyes wide and dark, biting her upper lip. "Why is it okay?" she asked.

"Oh, he's really safe with newbies," Joni said. "It's only when people think they know how to ride that he's bad. And I'll be leading him."

"No. I mean, why is it okay to *ride*?"

"Well—he lets me!" Joni said. "Archie's a lot stronger than I am. If he wasn't okay with me riding him, I wouldn't have a chance. I mean—" This was a serious question. What was the right thing to say, the *true* thing?

"He tries to get his own way all the time," she said. "It's a struggle. But it's like—we're equals. Sometimes I win, sometimes he wins, and we're both okay with that."

Chess was biting her lower lip now. "Okay," she said abruptly. "How do I get on?"

Joni tried not to look astonished. "You have to put this on first," she said, taking off her helmet. She helped Chess adjust it and explained how giving a leg up worked. Then she laced her fingers together to make a stirrup. Chess put her left knee into it.

"Grab his mane," Joni said.

"Won't that hurt him?"

"No, it's like—if you grab all your hair in one hand and pull, that doesn't hurt."

Chess reached up and tugged a fistful of her own hair. That hairstyle was looking a little scraggly these days, a little country.

"Okay." She took hold of Archie's mane, and, with Joni pushing, scrambled awkwardly onto his back.

"Scooch forward," Joni said. "Feel where his back dips a little? That's where he's strongest." She waited while Chess adjusted herself. "You ready?" Chess nodded. Joni started Archie walking. He had that soft look in his eyes, the way he did with little kids. He was taking care of Chess. "You're such an amazing horse!" Joni told him. How could he be so completely reliable when it mattered, and such a scamp the rest of the time? She looked back at Chess.

She was sitting very straight, fingers twined in Archie's mane, eyes large and shining. Joni stopped herself from saying anything. She just walked Archie quietly and steadily across the field and up to the barn. Olivia glanced out the window of the cheese house as they passed. Her eyes widened, and she gave Joni a thumbs-up. Chess didn't seem to notice that or anything else but Archie.

Joni stopped him beside the barn door. Chess looked down at her, still wordless. Joni hated to break the spell, but here they were. "Lean forward on his neck, swing your right leg across his back, and slide down," she said.

Still in a daze, Chess obeyed. She did it pretty well. Joni thought she'd probably done gymnastics, but this wasn't the time to ask.

On the ground, Chess put her arms around Archie's neck. He tossed his head, as he almost always did. Chess stepped back. "He doesn't like to be hugged?"

"Not really. I do it anyway." Joni met Chess's eyes. "I figure he can deal," she said, and Chess laughed.

TWENTY-SIX

"The Kid Who Saved Those Minis"

Saturday, the sun rose on a week of Archie. First, there was the drama of loading him into the borrowed horse trailer. Would he go on? Archie stretched the suspense to half an hour before suddenly pricking his ears and striding up the ramp. They picked up Danae and Pumpkin and were on their way to riding camp.

The equestrian center was a group of low brown stables among fields, with a brook winding through it. The Colts and Fillies were quartered on the brook side of C Barn this year. That was the best side, shady and cool even in the middle of the day. They set up their group tack stall, got the horses ready, and hurried off to their first classes.

Mrs. Abernathy's rule—look where you want the horse to

go—got Joni a surprised, admiring smile from Carleen and placement in the Intermediate class. She almost felt bad about that. Danae was still in Beginners, and Joni was the youngest in Western Intermediate.

But the older kids remembered her from last year, and word had spread. "Are you the kid who saved those minis?" people kept asking. She had stature.

Her riding got respect, too. For the first couple of days, when something like figure eights at the lope seemed too hard, the teenagers in her class kept saying, "You can do it, Joni!" That helped, but it helped even more to pretend she was Mrs. Abernathy. After a couple of days, nobody needed to encourage her anymore.

On Wednesday, Danae moved up to Intermediate, too. They were no longer the little kids. By the end of the summer, they would be teenagers, and at last they knew enough to actually do what the instructors were telling them. Finesse was possible. It happened every day.

Stable inspections were also better this year. Joni had passed on Mrs. Abernathy's secret, and none of their tack had even a speck of buckle gunk. Only Archie messed up their scores, with his habit of bringing mouthfuls of hay to the stall door and dribbling into the aisle while he ate.

"You could put up a stall guard to prevent that," the inspector suggested on the first day.

"But he wouldn't be able to look out," Joni said. "Archie lives by himself, so he likes to see other horses."

"I can only score you for Stable Keeping," the inspector said. "But as far as the welfare of the horse goes, I agree." Joni swept the aisle continually, and the others helped, too, but they couldn't catch every stray wisp of hay.

Late afternoons, back at the campground, the Colts and Fillies swam and helped cook supper over a real fire. Afterward, they lay on the camper bunks talking until they fell asleep. Even Tod talked. As the only Colt, he had a pup tent next to the camper. Willow started calling him "Pup," and from the moment he got a nickname, it seemed like he never shut up. And he was funny! Who knew? He would be in ninth grade next year, and Joni and Danae would be in seventh. They wouldn't have classes together, but maybe they'd see him in the hallways and say, "Hey, Pup!"

On Thursday night, Mom was campground parent. She brought lasagna made with sheep's milk cheese, and fresh farm eggs for breakfast, and they popped popcorn over the campfire. Joni learned that Chess had been to see the kittens every day.

Chess? Kittens? That all seemed like a long time ago.

But not totally. Sometimes Joni would look at a horse and the Chess question would pop into her head. "Does he *like* doing that?" The chestnut pony that kept refusing jumps. Nervous horses that fussed and champed at their bits, and pranced when they could have been walking. The lazy ones with riders who thumped their sides. She didn't think all of them liked what they were doing. Neither did all of the riders—but, of course, the riders got to choose, didn't they?

Probably—though Joni saw some of their parents in action, and she wasn't sure.

But Archie was certainly having fun. He loved being with other horses, and he nickered joyously every morning when

Joni came into sight. He was still Archie, with his own ways of doing things, like stopping to splash in the brook every time they crossed it, and trotting much faster than the poky Western jog the instructor wanted from them. Joni didn't mind that. When she got on, she wanted to go somewhere, not mince around a show ring to collect a blue ribbon. "Well, you're a happy camper!" the instructor said. It wasn't meant as a compliment, but Joni didn't care. She *was* a happy camper. That was one of the things she wasn't going to grow out of.

Then, in a snap of the fingers, it was Saturday. Mom came back for the end-of-camp horse show. She brought a whole cheering section—Dad, Olivia, Alyssa, Grandma DeeDee, even Rosita and Tobin. So many people, but Joni wanted more. "Did you guys ask Chess to come?" she asked as Olivia straightened her string tie for her.

Olivia nodded. "She couldn't face it."

Joni understood. The story of the minis had spread quickly. How did you walk into a place full of people who knew all about your biggest-ever mistake? And Joni wouldn't have been able to help her. Today, she had a horse show to ride in.

Last year, everyone said consoling things after the show and told Joni how proud they were that she'd gotten through a week of camp with a horse like Archie. This year, she didn't need consoling. Archie was game for everything and good at a lot of it, including jumping and barrel racing. He won several ribbons, and Joni got a mention at the closing ceremony for being especially improved.

All because of Mrs. Abernathy. Joni looked out at the crowd, wishing she could say that. And there was Mrs. Abernathy herself, straw hat and all!

But, *really*? She came all the way up for this? Not with Mom and Dad, either. She was far away from them, talking with one of the 4-H leaders, and she didn't catch Joni's eye, but she did look proud and satisfied.

Later, as Joni was packing her tack trunk, Mrs. Abernathy came walking along the row of stalls. She wasn't using her cane, and she wasn't limping much. Maybe she felt better. Or maybe she was too proud to limp around a bunch of horse people.

"That was excellent work." She caught hold of one end of Archie's saddle blanket to help Joni fold it. "You've made a lot of progress this week."

"Thank you," Joni said. "For coming, I mean."

"It's fun to reconnect with people," Mrs. Abernathy said. "And fun to see my pupil do so well. Do you want more lessons this summer? I'm happy to do it in exchange for eggs, or maybe a wedge of cheese once in a while."

Joni nodded, distracted. Pup had just said something funny. Everyone was laughing and Joni wanted to join in, to keep the camp feeling going.

But camp was o-o-o-o-ver, just like sixth grade. Home was real again all of a sudden, and there was something she needed to do.

"My friend Chess—" she began. Mrs. Abernathy's face stiffened.

"She didn't know," Joni said. "She didn't understand that grass could be bad for them. She's really sorry."

"I'd rather not discuss it," Mrs. Abernathy said.

"No, but—"

"It's the combination of ignorance and arrogance that I find so infuriating," Mrs. Abernathy said. "These people know absolutely nothing about animals, but they presume to tell those of us who do—"

"Chess knows a lot more already," Joni said. "And she's my friend."

Mrs. Abernathy started to answer. Then she stopped herself, looking sharply at Joni. "Are you saying if I don't forgive her, *we* can't be friends?"

That wasn't what Joni meant at all. She started to say that. Then she decided not to. She lifted her chin and looked straight at Mrs. Abernathy. It was one of the hardest things she'd ever done.

After a moment, Mrs. Abernathy said, "But I'm the grown-up. As you gently remind me." She tucked the saddle blanket into the space left for it at the corner of the tack trunk. Then she straightened.

"All right. Tell her to bake me another cake. I tasted a crumb of the first one, if the truth be told. It was good! Then she and I will duke it out and come to an understanding. Because *we* have to be friends, Joni. I insist on that."

"Me, too," Joni said.

But—*duke it out?* How much fun was *that* going to be?

Oh, well. She was "the kid who saved those minis," so she could probably deal.

TWENTY-SEVEN

Cake

Oh, groan! Joni thought, waking up on Sunday morning. Camp was over. What would she do all day? Who would she talk and laugh with?

Then she remembered. She was going to Chess's house to help bake the second cake and take it to Mrs. Abernathy. "I can't do it by myself," Chess had said, and Joni had decided not to mention Mrs. Abernathy's plan to "duke it out."

So that was who she'd talk with today. Laughing? Maybe not so much.

She checked on Archie. At home, he had his pasture and didn't need to be fed, but he seemed unusually glad to see her this morning. Did he miss camp, too? "You need a friend," Joni told him. Not that she needed another horse to ride, but Archie had been so happy hanging out over his stall door. It wasn't fair to make him live alone.

And so many horses needed homes. Maybe she could adopt somebody from Kalysta's. Like Patrick? He and Archie would look cute together, like salt and pepper shakers.

But Hooper needed a home more. He might never be rideable. Someone would have to take care of him . . . and did Joni want to be a horse's caretaker for years and years? She felt bad even thinking that. Maybe Mom and Dad wouldn't let her adopt a horse. No point in getting all agonized about which one to choose before she even knew that.

Back in the house, Rosita was making French toast while Mom sat peacefully with her coffee and notebook. Dad came in from the barn, leaving Tobin and Olivia to do cleanup. "Hey, Joni Macaroni! I missed you!"

"I didn't miss you," Joni said. "But I love you!" she added, as his eyebrows popped up. "I was just having so much fun."

"I get it," Dad said, sounding a bit regretful. Joni gave him a hug.

They were eating by the time Olivia came in from the barn with Tobin. They kicked off their boots, and Joni saw them kiss quickly before coming to the table and sitting far apart from each other as if nothing had changed. She met Rosita's eyes. They both tried not to laugh, and Olivia said, "*What?*" Tobin blushed. Cute! Joni wondered if there was a way to make Pup blush.

Mountains of French toast vanished, and the platter of bacon had to be guarded from the kittens. They were big enough now to climb people's legs and old enough to be driven to a frenzy by new, great-smelling foods. Finally, Joni corralled them in her room. Their pathetic mews reached all the way to the breakfast table. "Cruel!" Mom commented, and Joni thought of Chess. And Mrs. Abernathy. She reached for a fourth slice of French toast. She would need her strength today.

After breakfast, she went out and saddled Archie. He turned to look at her as she tightened the girth, as if to say, *Really?* "I know," Joni said. "This will be easy, though."

She felt guilty as she climbed onto the big rock to mount. She had sore muscles, so Archie probably did, too. He really should have today off. But he lined himself up to let her get on, which he didn't always do even when perfectly rested. "Thank you," Joni said, and gave him a vigorous neck scratch before setting off.

She rode at a walk across the field. At a walk along the shady brook trail. At a hollowly thudding walk across the wooden bridge and onto North Valley Road.

Chess waited beside the roadside paddock. She'd mowed it with a lawnmower and raked out the grass clippings as Joni had instructed, so it was safe for Archie. Joni unsaddled him and turned him loose. He put his head down, took a nip of the very short grass, and ripped out a disgusted sigh.

Chess chuckled. "'Where's the stinkin' grass?' Right? Is that what he was saying?"

"Yup." Joni checked Archie's water pail—full, and tied to a post with baling twine. Chess was learning fast.

"Wow! I understood him!" Chess said. "I know what the kittens are saying sometimes, too."

"This morning, they were saying *'Ba-a-a-a-con!* Give us *ba-a-a-a-con!'*"

Chess looked alarmed. "Do I have to feed them bacon?"

"What do you mean, 'them'?"

"Didn't your mom tell you? We're taking two," Chess said.

"What happened to 'no captive animals'?" Joni asked.

Chess said, "I've decided it's not wrong. At least, *I* don't think so. Not if you take good care of them. That's why we're taking two. Cats like to have another cat around, even if they don't seem to be friends. That's what I read, anyway."

Chess would take better care of those kittens than anyone in the history of cats! Joni was sure of that. "What about your grandmother?"

"We're talking about it," Chess said. "She still doesn't think it's right, but she loves animals, so maybe she'll change her mind when she meets them."

Chess's grandmother didn't sound like the kind of person who ever changed her mind—but Joni had thought that about Chess. "So, this cake," she asked, as they crossed the road. "Is it the one you brought to graduation?"

Chess nodded. "She *ate* a piece? Off the ground?" Joni shrugged. It was possible. Mrs. Abernathy was a surprising lady. "It's vegan," Chess said. "Should we tell her?"

"No!" Joni said. "Let's just hope she doesn't ask for the recipe! By the way—you know cats aren't vegetarians, right?"

"They're obligate carnivores," Chess said. "That means they have to eat meat." She met Joni's eyes. "I'm *never* eating an animal, Joni. That's not going to change just because I have cats!"

"Okay," Joni said. No point asking about eggs or cheese. She had a feeling they might never be able to trade sandwiches at lunchtime—but so what!

In the kitchen, she read the list of dry ingredients from the cake recipe while Chess measured them into a bowl. The house was quiet. "Where is everybody?" Joni asked.

"Mom's in the garden. Dad and Noah went to church."

That's right, it was Sunday. The 4-Hers who hadn't gone to camp were taking their turn at Kalysta's. "I wonder how Hooper and Patrick are," Joni said.

"Who are they, boys at camp?"

"No, horses at the rescue. Hooper has founder and Patrick was starved. Hooper started some new medicine last week. I wonder if it's helping."

"Is there a website?" Chess asked. "Maybe she posted something."

"Oh! I think she has one. I've never looked."

Chess dusted flour off her hands and went to the front window where a slender laptop computer rested on an elegant stand. "You guys won't be able to leave that there when you have kittens," Joni said. The Venturas had a lot to learn!

Chess's fingers danced over the keys. "Here it—oh, *no!*"

Joni wasn't surprised to see a picture of Patrick filling the screen. His ribs pushed against his dull coat. Vertebrae knuckled up at his withers. Joni looked away quickly, concentrating on what Kalysta had written under the picture.

In spite of everything, Patrick retains his trust in human beings. One of my volunteers called him "a grown-up," and he is. A grown-up, and a gentleman.

Patrick needs a forever home. Once he's regained his strength, he will be able to be ridden and enjoyed. In the meantime, we are looking for someone who can offer this wonderful horse a foster home for a few months. He needs supervised grazing and lots of sunshine. Patrick has a whole year's worth of attention and love to make up for.

I could give him that! Joni thought. *I could. I'll ask Mom and—*

"Who can be a foster home?" Chess asked in a strangled voice.

Joni felt her scalp tingle. She hesitated, choosing her words carefully. "Kalysta checks people out. She asks for references and makes sure they know about horses."

"I don't know anything. And I stole . . ." Chess swallowed. "Could I at least take him some grass?"

"You mean, *pick* him some?" Joni had picked grass for horses. It was crazy! What seemed like a huge handful disappeared down the horse's throat in seconds, and then it wanted more. "Come meet him," she said. "Talk to Kalysta!"

Kalysta would ask the same question. *Pick him grass? How much grass do you have?* Joni looked out at the broad fields across the road.

How much grass? Plenty. Plenty to carefully fatten a very thin horse, plenty left to make into hay and store in the barn for winter. Plenty to help start a hay bank, even . . .

Archie whinnied. He stood with his head high, staring up North Valley Road. Joni heard a muffled rattle and squeak.

A moment later, the minis trotted into view, brisk and bouncy. Their tiny ears swiveled, and their manes floated on the breeze they made. Over their front hooves, they wore bright slip-on boots. Kubota's were orange, JD's green and yellow.

Behind them, Mrs. Abernathy sat large and upright in the cart. She wore a straw hat with a wild turkey feather sticking up jauntily from the band. As she passed, she looked toward the kitchen window and lifted her whip to touch the brim of her hat. Then she turned her face toward the bridge. The wheels spun her around the corner out of sight.

Joni would still have been babying the minis, but probably exercise was best. Mrs. Abernathy must know.

And she would know the answer to any horse question a newbie neighbor might ask. *Any* question.

It was going to take cake, though. A lot of cake.

Jessie Haas has written more than thirty-five books, most of them about horses. Her novels include *Shaper*, which won a Golden Kite Honor Award; *Unbroken*, which was a *Publishers Weekly* Best Book, a *School Library Journal* Best Book, and a CCBC Choice, among other honors; and *Chase*. She lives in Vermont with her husband, two horses, two cats, and a dog. Visit jessiehaas.com.